THE GHOST OF SQUIRE MCDERMOTT

RICHARD LIGHT

Copyright © 2026 by Richard Light

All rights reserved.
No part of this book may be reproduced in any form or by any electronic or mechanical means, including information storage and retrieval systems, without written permission from the author, except for the use of brief quotations in a book review.

This is a work of fiction. Unless otherwise indicated, all the names, characters, businesses, places, events and incidents in this book are either the product of the author's imagination or used in a fictitious manner. Any resemblance to actual persons, living or dead, or actual events is purely coincidental.

For more information email: richardlightauthor@gmail.com

ISBN (hardcover): 979-8-89571-322-8
ISBN (ebook): 979-8-89571-323-5
ISBN (paperback): 979-8-89571-321-1

R7L Publishing
Success Publications Sar

CHAPTER 1

"Call me Mason," the well-dressed, young attorney said as he leaned back in his chair. He was supposed to be the best when it came to odd occurrences – a cool head when things got weird. He certainly looked unmoved and relaxed as his shoes came up to rest. There was not a speck of dirt on the soles nor look of surprise on Mason Braddock Esquire's face. "Have you ever been sued before, Mr. McDermott?"

"No, first time," Squire replied. "I don't really understand this."

"It looks like you have been caught up in the rebirth of an era long gone. In the old days, it was called Alienation of Affection or its ugly cousin Criminal Conversation. That's obviously a euphemism. At the time, there were a few states that considered it a real crime, either a felony or a misdemeanor depending on the locale and circumstances. But that's all a moot point now with the new focus on family values laws most of the conservative states are adopting. Here it's called the Family Unity Sustainment Act.

"Whatever they want to call it – lewd and lascivious behavior it is. It's my opinion that most everyone likes to either get themselves involved in it or, at the minimum, think about it. To fantasize, so to speak," Mason Braddock Esquire laughed. "What are they calling it on social media? The Punish Alpha Law? That sort of makes this husband the beta by default doesn't it?"

"I don't really know. I am not sure where beta and alpha begin and end," Squire frowned. "All I did was sleep with her a couple times. I didn't know she was married."

"Well, her husband did... And according to this, you kept sleeping with her after you found out. There was more to her than a poke, wasn't there?"

Squire looked more crestfallen than ashamed.

* * *

STEPHEN ROGERS SAT REMEMBERING how they met, at an annual fraternity party. She was everything he dreamt about. Through the haze of his beer goggles he approached, stumbling closer. She was so pretty. Four minutes before he would puke his eyes inside out, he fumbled with his phone and got her number. A fraternity brother pulled him away, ushering Stephen up the stairs before the vomit volcano began to erupt.

He awoke around 8:00 a.m., his head pounding, soothed only by the cool of the toilet tank. He smelled of piss and puke but as his coherence improved so did his memory. Did he really talk to her? That girl, the nurse? Did she say she was a nurse? He searched for his phone, finding it lodged between the sink pedestal and the wall. He had managed to fumble off a message: *Hey, let's g out somtim*

OK, let's, she replied.

It took longer than he expected to get her out on a date

but three kids later, over 15 years and she did this. It wasn't her, not his Meagan. And with a fucking bartender... The guilt he felt for recording her came and went between fits of rage, thoughts of revenge, and self-pity. The way she cried when he played the recording...

Jen, thank God I wasn't. Can you imagine? I was just a little late. Oh my God, what did I do? I have to tell Stephen...

NO! No you don't. That's not going to help. Just forget him and don't go back to that bar, ever.

"Why?" Stephen yelled. He couldn't get the image of it out of his head as he confronted her. "What did you do? You fucked a bartender? We barely have sex anymore and you fucked *him*! I heard the whole conversation! You never fucked me like that!"

"I don't know what happened to me," Meagan cried. "He manipulated me somehow."

* * *

"This complaint has some nice adjectives: debaucherous, lecherous, salacious. Are you really all of these things? Do you prey on women?" Mason asked.

"I don't know," Squire sighed, "maybe."

"No, you don't," Mason corrected him. "And starting now, you don't do interviews. You don't talk to anyone without me around."

"I don't think that's a problem," Squire replied. "I can either be or not be at work. They don't seem to notice."

"That might be a symptom of your condition. Besides, didn't they fire you when they found out?"

Squire sighed again. They sent the prettiest waitress to tell him; the one who saw him for what he was. He begged her to ask management to reconsider but they all just stared like they were looking right through him. Husbands and boyfriends started showing up flexing everything they had. The place was turning rough. He had to go. He found a place that would take him but only to make drinks for the seated guests from a bar hidden away from wives then another bar that hadn't heard about him yet.

"I didn't know she was married," Squired lamented. "I was really surprised she was married to *him*."

Mason paused to think. He could see the confusion. Stephen Rogers was a private equity manager, sort of squishy but not completely fat, bearded. He was married to an well-above average looking woman, at least a seven, church-going, thin, gregarious, great mom, hair suspiciously blond. They had a nice house, a nice life. He had everything a young man enters college hoping to obtain and he did it all with a freshly printed MBA. *If Squire had slept with my wife*, Mason thought, *if I had one…*

"Were you always single?" Mason asked.

Squires eyes dropped. He had no idea why he had never married. Frustrating endings, one after the other and he still didn't know what the problem was. He tried everything they said he should do to keep a woman. He went slow. He went to church. He went to the bookstore, the coffee shop. He tried to be aloof. He tried to be sensitive. He tried to wine and dine. He tried to meet the families. He tried to be friends first. He tried just being himself. Nothing worked. He got them and failed at keeping them. It seemed like something he could fix so he kept on hoping. "I tried everything, even celibacy," he replied.

Mason laughed, "How long did that last?"

"A couple of months, I was pretty good at it." A smile cracked on Squire's face remembering his forced abstinence. It wasn't in his nature to ignore women nor in theirs to ignore him. What he really meant by abstinence was seclusion.

Something seemed to draw them in, something otherworldly. He didn't know if it was a need or just his way of being. It didn't help that he had just enough good looks to get attention from a lot of women. Too huge of a discrepancy in appearance and the woman would ignore him. If she was too hot, she would have other opportunities, other agendas. Too plain and they wouldn't even look at him unless there were drinks involved. The ones who really saw him were always pretty, sometimes cute.

"I didn't know she was married," Squire mumbled.

"Yeah," Mason interrupted, "you said that. You didn't ask?"

"It just escalated so quickly."

"You mean she was a same-day-lay? One night stand?" Mason's eyes narrowed. Some of these clients... This one was different. This case was different. Defending idiots against the results of their urges as their wives sought to destroy them was one thing, but in front of him sat the destroyer – the scapegoat for a man on the warpath, Stephen Rogers. They were going to dig up everyone they could from Squire's past. "Ever sleep with a girl who had a boyfriend?"

"Without a doubt," Squire shot back almost too quickly for Mason's liking.

"So you don't have a problem being the other man," Mason replied.

Squired stalled. Mason stared at him impatiently. "How do I say this?" Squire shifted. "If you want her, put a ring on her and get the deed done. That being said, I am not a predator. I don't go after attached women. I just like women. Seriously, who doesn't? Why am I being sued? Why me?"

"Exactly," Mason said as he looked up at Squire. "Why you? That's what we're going to find out and I don't believe for a minute that they will settle out of court. They'll want to. They will want to mediate this for a lot of reasons, one in particular is avoiding the stand, and publicity, and the jury. They'll want you to submit, to cave in, and repent then they'll evaporate this problem into thin air and into their bank accounts. I would plan on this going to trial if I were you. You and I have a lot to talk about between now and then…"

CHAPTER 2

The plaintiffs and opposing attorney entered, puffed up and ready. The icy glare from Stephen Rogers was enough to know the damages sought would be excessive. And now a Motion to Amend dropped on the table before them – the addition of another plaintiff... Mason and Squire sat silently across the table listening to the demands.

"Well that didn't go well," Mason muttered as they walked into their caucus room. Squire paced remembering...

"So, that's him...," he sighed, "I never believed the description until now."

"I think I know what you mean," Mason grinned. "You expected more?"

"Yeah, you should have seen how quickly she forgot about me," Squire replied. "I expected something more than that."

* * *

"Hi, what can I get you?" he asked as she glanced up. Her eyes rounded soulfully. He knew the look.

"Um, I'm supposed to meet some friends here. Maybe I should wait."

She was pretty. Her dark roots were only millimeters long under the blond – a fresh color. "Wine while you wait?" he asked.

"Whatever the house white is," she smiled up at him. It had been a long time since a man looked at her like this. Suddenly she felt desired. Something stirred in her. Her husband tried hard to do these things at a regular, almost methodical pace. But it was another world when a guy like this one reacted to her.

Her husband seemed to know just when to ask, when she was at her weakest. He never seemed to care about whether she was mechanical, uninspired, attending to his needs with just enough affection. Everything seemed to come second to him but she knew it was unintentional. He was trying. He tried all the time, but he would never really understand and she had no way to put what she felt into the right words. The frantic thrusts followed by, "Did you finish?" he would ask as if waiting for a barrage of accolades. What could she say?

A half-hour passed, the cute bartender refilled without her consent. She accepted. To be here with him, away from the house was all she wanted.

"Where are your friends? Do you have any friends?" he teased.

She laughed. The way he said it. She could tell he saw through the story; there were no friends coming. Was it so obvious? She felt herself caught up watching him polish glasses, holding them up to the light for inspection. It seemed masterful, ethereal how the light seemed to make him and the wineglasses luminesce. He caught her watching. She blushed.

"Do you have french fries?" she asked.

"There are french fries here," he grinned. He waited, their

eyes met again. She lost her sense of time. With a deep breath, he leaned forward. "Tell me what you want…"

"French fries," the words escaped her lips.

Squire sensed her vulnerability. He turned away towards the kitchen. *She is really pretty*, he thought. The cooks were in the alley getting high. He helped himself to a freshly made batch arranging them in a way befitting her.

"Wow," she exclaimed, "that's fancy." An array of stainless steel sauce cups complimented the fries.

"Frites et une variété de sauces pour mademoiselle," he grinned and turned away. She was hooked. A couple came in and dropped into seats nearby.

"Squire!" the man said as he reached over the bar to shake hands. The woman stepped behind the bar for a hug. Meagan watched the adoration they had for this handsome, unassuming man. He seemed to flow naturally in his space, uninhibited and without pretense. It was obvious from his physique that he worked out, everything about him looked strong. She caught herself wondering how his strong hands would feel on her. She shook herself back into the fog of her reality but every time she looked up at him the sun burst through.

What am I doing? she thought. She hadn't felt these things in years. A random Tuesday, the prelude to Happy Hour and she was at a bar drinking wine, eating frites – a word she remembered from high school French. *How much younger is he?* she wondered as she looked down at her bare ring finger. *Five years, maybe?* Her phone buzzed: *How's it going? Pookie OK?*

He's at the vet, she texted. *He's going to be fine. Don't worry.*

OK, love you. We're having a really good time here.

As the french fries disappeared she knew she should force herself to get up and walk out, but something anchored her. The woman asked her where she was from as the husband continued to talk to Squire. The admiration the man had, as if he lived vicariously through him. It was respect; it was obvious.

That smile he has, she thought. *It's a little devious.* The woman kept bouncing back and forth between the men's conversation and questions for Meagan. She caught the subtle attraction the woman had for Squire; as if it were not for the husband, there would be all out girl-war between them. Meagan found herself daydreaming about it, pulling hair and scratching like they were impassioned teenagers. She had never been one of them. Those kinds of girls seemed like they charged ahead for what they wanted. She had always done what she should, expecting more than what came along. When she diverged from *should* she lost her chance to choose, too young to remember what it was like.

"You and Squire would look really good together," Meagan heard the woman interject into her wandering thoughts.

"Excuse me?" Meagan replied.

"You. And Squire...," she replied. She leaned in to whisper, "He is so hot."

Meagan wanted to respond but the words didn't come out. She had had her chance to free herself and run, to take the path prescribed and safe but something told her to stay on this one, wandering deep into the woods. Something inside her screamed to feel what it would be like to risk everything.

* * *

THE MEDIATOR ENTERED, document in hand. Squire looked at Mason who gestured for him to sit as he took the papers. Mason's brow furrowed as he read. Squire watched Mason mouth, *one hundred thousand*. A sudden pulse of dread hit him. What did that mean? Mason slid the document across the table.

One hundred thousand dollars. It was right there. He would admit liability and pay it. Simple as that. He sat stunned. The reality of the lawsuit glared up at him. *I can't pay that*, his head raced. He looked frantically at Mason, shaking his head.

"It's not on this document," the mediator said, "but Mr. Rogers' attorney says he has another plaintiff. You got the Motion to Amend."

"Oh, fuck that guy," Mason yelled. The mediator recoiled indignantly at Mason's lack of professionalism.

"You don't agree," the mediator said calmly. "Do you have a counter offer?"

"Our counter is nothing," Mason grumbled. "The plaintiff's wife seduced him. Tell that chump that and tell him he should be paying one hundred thousand to my client for finally giving her an orgasm. We'll only charge him for one."

The mediator looked shocked as if she had never heard such disrespect coming out of an attorney. "I'm not telling them that."

"Then tell them, no thanks. See ya later," Mason growled. "Whatever they want above five dollars is an insult to us. Even then, we won't admit liability."

"Their marriage is in shambles," the mediator tried to reason. "Your client admitted to the affair in a text to the plaintiff."

Mason scowled at Squire. He was tired of scolding him for that error. If people would just learn to shut the fuck up once in a while, he could live in poverty, contented, perhaps do something useful with his life. Was it ego? Was that it? Did Squire have to out himself for some sort of self-absorbed pat on the back? "Everyone's a fucking idiot sometimes," he muttered.

Squire tried to keep up as Mason stomped out ahead spewing obscenities. *What kind of lawyers is this?* he wondered. In the parking garage Mason's demeanor took a full reversal. He began to laugh. "What?" Squire asked.

"I know this mediator pretty well. She is great but she thinks I am a total wing-nut and she has no poker face," Mason continued to laugh. "She won't tell them anything I said but it will be all over that face of hers."

"You didn't want to counter?" Squire asked.

"No," Mason replied, "they were trying to scare us."

"What happens now?"

Mason grinned, "They give up or we go to court." He let the comment sit as he studied Squire's reaction. "I want to go to court and, trust me, you do too."

* * *

HIS PHONE SLID across the bar coming to stop next to her red manicured nails. "You seem pretty cool. We should hang out sometime."

She looked up at him and, without a thought, keyed in her number. In the car on the way home her emotions ran wild. "How? How can I?" she lectured herself. "Maybe just like he said, hang out some time. Like friends. Or maybe just text for a while then I'll block him."

The wall of denial she began to build crumpled; she rebuilt it over and over as she pulled into the garage to an eerily quiet house. It was three more weeks until Stephen and the kids would be back from Rhode Island. She could picture his entrance: wearing a light blue, striped button down and khakis for the plane, the kids following behind, dragging bags and grumbling about going back to school. He would kiss her on the cheek. Behind the touch of his hands, his belly would be next in line to touch her. Was it so difficult for an accountant to workout? *Private equity*, she corrected herself, *not an accountant*. He just seemed like one, whatever that seemed like.

For some reason she chose a black silk negligee for the night. The TV streamed a romantic comedy she heard was good. The sound was off, unnecessary for what she had in mind. Her hands ran up and down her body preparing herself, her mind. The phone buzzed.

Hey, it was him. He didn't need to say much more than that. She watched the typing bubble pulsate.

Meet me for a drink. A chat.
Now? she replied.
Now
Where?

* * *

Where is he? Meagan asked herself as she stepped into the bar. The lobby of the boutique hotel was impeccably postmodern, slightly over-exaggerated. It wasn't in line with the vibe she had gotten from him hours before. It left her a little overwhelmed; or maybe it was the whole scene. What was she doing there? What propelled her? She could have been satisfied just to stay in, wrapped up in her sheets with her movie and a fantasy.

She caught a hint of him. As she spun around, he was walking towards her, reaching out his hand to take hers. A handshake? It lingered, the feeling of him touching her. The fingers slipped away from each other then held on as if they were clutching desperately to save the other from a fall. "Come on," he said as he led her to the corner of a dark bar in a darker pub. "Cosmopolitan?" he asked.

Her eyes lit up, her head shook affirmatively. How did he know? The bartender joined them.

"Cosmo," he said, "and a Macallen 12 neat." As the bartender took up his shaker, Squire turned to her, "How are you?"

Meagan paused, her eyes glittered. For whatever reason she felt calm near him, but not without a hint of an anxious feeling she could barely remember feeling years before. She wanted to be talkative but didn't know what to say. Then, it all seemed to pour out of her in fewer words than she had ever used with a man, "I am really good right now," she answered. "How are you?"

"Excellent," Squire smiled.

That little grin of his. It was too natural to be rehearsed. Her hand came up to her hair, brushing it back behind an ear. His hand gently brushed away something from her cheek. An eyelash? She didn't ask. The gentle touch answered everything.

"This is a really nice bar," Meagan said, steering the wordless conversation they were having towards something tangible.

A little laugh escaped him as he leaned back. The distance between them grew. Meagan didn't know how to respond. Had she killed the moment between them? The drinks arrived. The bartender seemed unfocused as he the cosmopolitan in front of Squire, the Scotch in front of her. Squire gently picked up the chilled martini glass and held it, "Cheers," he grinned.

Meagan responded with the Scotch. "Cheers," she laughed.

He was funny, unassuming, unfazed as he sipped the cosmo with a full pinky extension before setting it in front of her. At that moment, it seemed as though they had known each other for years.

"What did you do that you are proud of today?" he asked.

"I went out all by myself," Meagan laughed.

"And how'd that go?"

"So, far...really good," she replied, her teeth clenched a little over her lower lip. She felt his foot rest on her stool. Her foot slid near. They talked like old friends who secretly wanted each other, forever waiting for the right moment. Finally the moment had come when they could be alone together, their feet meeting in a choreographed dance of innocent foreplay before the distant culmination of their desires. He said something funny, her hand playfully slapped his leg and paused. His hand covered hers, fingers intertwined. They stayed like this as people came and went. Then a pause... Eyes met, his hand came up behind her head, in the silence, her lips slipped open as they met his.

* * *

"That's it?" Mason asked as he dropped into his desk chair. "That's how it happened?"

"Yeah, that's how I met her," Squire recalled as he sank into his chair, remembering the good times with Meagan took it out of him. He had to reach back in for them against his will. Almost all of it seemed destined to put him in a place he should find contentment, even the day she finally told him. Married. He was too hooked by then...

"So, how long before sex?" Mason asked as he looked up from his legal pad. Squire hesitated. "Just give me a ballpark."

"Fifteen maybe twenty minutes after we left the bar," Squire remembered.

"Fifteen, twenty minutes? Jesus Christ," Mason exclaimed. "Bullshit!"

"No, it was pretty fast," Squire assured him.

Mason looked at Squire, searching for signs. It was obvious he was telling the truth. He was a pro at spotting the lies. This guy was being completely upfront, like he had no ego investment to fortify. Squire was just what he was; but it seemed as though he was the only one who didn't know who that was. It was at that moment Mason knew the problem he faced. The trial was going to open a box of mayhem for the women and men involved.

"Where?" Mason asked.

"Where what?"

"Where did you sleep with her?"

"At my place," Squire responded. His memory ran through the scene.

* * *

"Where's your car?" Meagan asked as he drew her near, wrapping his coat around her.

"I walked. My place is close by."

"Want a ride home?" she smiled as her hand lay gently on his chest.

"Sure..."

"If I come up, I am going to sleep with you," Meagan blushed.

"Don't be silly. I'm not that kind of boy. A glass of wine, then I kick you out."

CHAPTER 3

"Ladies and gentlemen of the jury," Woodrow P. Devine began. "The case you are about to hear is one of willful and lustful destruction of our most precious of institutions, marriage. My clients, Mr. and Mrs. Stephen and Meagan Rogers and Mr. and Mrs. Howard and Victoria Cullen, all shared long, happy relationships until a fateful meeting with the defendant, Mr. Squire McDermott.

"We will show that Mr. McDermott is a predator on the hunt searching for the slightest chink in the armor of loving, nurturing, and affectionate unions. Through his skills as, what has come to be known as pickup artistry, Mr. McDermott wheeled and dealed malevolence against the foundations of sacred oaths my clients took in front of family and almighty God to love and cherish each other until death do they part.

"It will be proven through salacious text messages, clandestine meetings, and utter depravity that Mr. Squire McDermott used his ill-gotten techniques to enrapture and ensnare the unsuspecting, innocent mothers and brides you see here before you. And there will be more…

"We will demonstrate a pattern of behavior spanning over a decade through witness testimony that Mr. McDermott is a patterned offender of innocence resulting in the breakdown of what we all hold close to our hearts. What's more, Mr. Squire McDermott has engaged in this behavior nearly his entire life. He is and will be proven to be a womanizer, a misogynist, and a sexual deviant who cannot control his most basic urges.

"His actions, and his actions alone, will be enough for you to see through the charade the defense plans to unleash upon you. His actions drove a wedge of doubt and suspicion into my clients that can never be repaired. His actions, still to this day, stand on the neck of the love and affection they once shared together constricting the air that breathes life into their lives.

"In the end, when you make your judgement, we will ask that you hold Mr. McDermott accountable for the damages he has caused. We will ask that you hold him accountable and reward my clients, Mr. and Mrs. Rogers and Cullen, with justice."

* * *

"WHAT ARE you talking about back there?"

"Nothing, Squire. Just take me home and lay me in bed, then fuck me until I sleep," Victoria mumbled. Drool ran down the side of her face mixed with blood.

"Hey," Howard Cullen yelled, "the seats! Use the towel!"

"Spank me with the towel Squire and tell me you love my tits. I had them made just for you. I'll call you papacito, como te gusta. Mi amoorrrr..."

Howard squinted at her in the rearview mirror. What was she talking about? Squire? The dentist must have drugged the hell out of her. *Squire... What a stupid name*, Howard thought as he pulled into the garage. *Must be some romance book asshole.* She squirmed around batting at the door handle as he opened it for her, catching her halfway out. Half dragging, half carrying her, he struggled towards the kitchen. "Oh yeah, Squire," Victoria giggled. "I want you to take me from behind like you used to. I'll bend over the counter. I'm so sorry I hurt you. Just fuck me. I'm a bad, bad girl."

Howard dropped the towel then his wife on the bed. He stood over her as she squirmed her way towards the pillow. Her hand ran over her breasts and down between her legs as she moaned out the name, Squire.

She can sleep off whatever delusions this character put in her, Howard thought. His wife curled herself into a ball, tears rolled down her cheeks as Howard dimmed the lights.

"The dentist said it would take a couple hours to move through her system but she'll be fine by morning," Howard muttered. He looked at the clock, he could make it to his meeting. As he backed out of the garage he looked into their bedroom window and wondered, could Squire be real? Maybe an old boyfriend from Colombia? But the boob job was only a few years old…

* * *

SQUIRE LOOKED OVER AT VICTORIA. She was still beautiful, staring straight ahead, her eyebrows crinkled together like she was about to unleash hell on someone. He hadn't seen that look in over 2 years. How could their fling have caused anything in her marriage? Another one who lied to him, then came clean, then lied about leaving her husband, then didn't, then dumped him and went back to hide somewhere in the upper middle class. Both of these women pursued him until…

God, who else do they have? he wondered as he scratched at a legal pad Mason had given him. Halfway through a sketch, he realized he was drawing a scene from the day he met Victoria.

It was Happy Hour at the bar; a group of women entered. They were all dressed up but not in corporate, just out of work, attire. As they took a hightop table, he overheard them talking about the matinée of *Les Misérables*, how beautiful it had been... *"to love another person is to see the face of God,"* the women all said in unison as she glanced across the bar at him.

His soul was taken from him. She held it in her hand at that moment. Every chance she had, their eyes met; those big, brown gorgeous eyes were calling him. Her fingers ran up and down the stem of her wine glass massaging it slowly as those eyes began to fixate on him. The way she tipped her head, acting like she was listening to her friends, while she fondled her neck...

When the waitress delivered the check, she snatched it up refusing anything from her friends. She scribbled the tip before shooing the other women out. As she stepped out the door, she tossed a flirtatious smile over her shoulder. "Wow," Squire remembered whispering as the waitress handed him the server book. "What?" he asked.

The waitress gave him an indignant tsk, "You know what... Look. Again?"

"You are hot, call me," the signature line said. Her number was local; her name, Victoria Restrepo, was printed under the signature line. "Did she tip you?" he asked. The waitress held up a fifty. "You can't be pissed about that," he said as the waitress spun on her heels towards an awaiting table.

* * *

"Mr. Braddock," the judge said giving Mason the floor.

Mason stood, adjusted his suit coat, and strolled calmly forward towards the jury. "Ladies and gentlemen, you have come here to perform your civic duty in the pursuit of justice. You should feel honored that you have been chosen for this trial in this courtroom." An almost inaudible groan emitted from Woodrow P. Devine. Squire saw the judge's head snap towards the plaintiffs' table. With a blank, serious demeanor, Woodrow P. Devine adjusted his tie.

"The plaintiffs are certainly in pain. Their marital problems have caused them much emotional harm but my client is no sexual deviant as Mr. Devine would like you to believe. He is a normal man, with normal male urges. But what the opposing side won't tell you is that he seeks love, affection, and the bonding the plaintiffs took for granted. As they say, it takes two to tango." The gallery began to laugh; a few of the jury members struggled to remain serious.

Judge Perkins gave the whole room a stern glare. "Carry on counsel," he muttered.

"My client is a rare example of a man and he is wrongly accused. When an attractive woman approaches him, he does what all men do. He was approached. He was deceived. The evidence will show this; and you, in accordance with justice, will exonerate him and return to your private lives better for having done what is right and what the spirit of justice put its faith in you to do."

Woodrow P. Devine's head rested in his palm. If not for the judge, he would have planted a hand on his forehead and yelled, "Bullshit!"

"When the evidence is put before you, your decision will be easy and just," Mason said as he sat down next to Squire.

Judge Perkins addressed the jury, "Through the course of the trial, evidence will be presented to you. Your duty is to decide on that evidence. These opening statements are not intended to sway your opinions either way."

Squire caught Victoria's gaze. He remembered her acting talents too well. Today, she was against him. She was preserving the subtle leverage she held over her husband but Squire knew another Victoria.

*   *   *

YOU GAVE me your number

Victoria glanced at the text. What took him so long? Two days seemed too long but there he was. He finally showed up. She wondered if she had made a mistake. There was more than looking good to being a man. She typed, *I'm on a flight back from LA squashed between two bellies with stubby necks, holding up beards. It's about time you texted. I was starting to wonder...*

Squire hesitated. She seemed informal, chatty with him like they were friends.

Slip your hand on the man's inner thigh who is sitting next to the aisle.

I'M NOT DOING THAT!!!!! HA! HA!

You can do it. He'll have to go to the bathroom.

OMG! For what?

Only he knows. When he's gone swap seats with him.

You are awful!!

Squire laughed. He could have just told her she was pretty and she could use it against her seat mates, but she knew she was pretty.

Where are these guys going? Chat them up. Make them believe you will meet them somewhere, both of them.

A ménage??? NO!!!

Yes!

NO!

He laid back against the pillows laughing. This woman

was fun already. Was she smart? Time would tell. For now she was hot.

What are you wearing?
You know, normal, she replied.
Normal how? Low cut normal? High heels? Pajamas?
Kinda low cut blouse and leggings.
Leggings
What's wrong with leggings?
You know what's wrong with leggings.
Tell me.

Squire hesitated, letting the leggings conversation wisp away into the clouds.

Can you imagine what they are thinking about you? he diverted.
No what? Tell me. What are you thinking?
I have horrible thoughts about you.
Horrible?
Scandalous
Oooooo, tell me
I really shouldn't. You can't handle it.
I can handle anything. TELL ME!!!!
OK, take a deep breath...

Squire gave her a moment to calm down. He knew nothing about this woman other than she was female and right now he assumed she was into him.

Are you there??? she asked.
I'm standing behind you. He paused to watch the screen. There was no indication she was typing.
It's dark in the room and you and I are together.
My hand slides around your wasted pulling you against me
Your hips begin to sway to the quiet music coming from the other room
We say nothing. Our bodies move together
I can feel you rub against me, making me want you

He waited. Still no indication. She was transfixed. He laughed as he visualized her descending into the fantasy between the two bellies with beards.

There is nothing but us

My hand moves up to take your breast as my lips find your neck

Your ass pushes hard against me, moving up and down to the music

Your hand reaches down and runs up the inside of your leg

My lips lock on to your neck, my hands both play with your breasts.

OMG you have to stop!!!

Squire laughed. An image of her about to masturbate in the middle seat flashed through his mind.

When can I see you? she asked.

When you're back

I am back tonight.

What time?

11, where do you live?

By the beach

So do I

The pause between them was heavy with anticipation.

Will you play the music? In the other room?

Yes

11:20 his doorbell rang. She stepped in. He took her by the hips and kissed her. It seemed frantic as they struggled to stay upright in his kitchen finally leveraging themselves against the counter. She yanked at his shirt. A button flew across the room bouncing on the tile. Finally they found his bed. In the morning, after too many times to remember he slipped into the bathroom and she slipped out. He knew her name. Somehow she knew his. He didn't remember telling her.

CHAPTER 4

"ou may call your first witness," Judge Perkins said as Woodrow P. Devine approached the lectern.

"Your Honor, I call Paige Brock to the stand as my first witness."

Brock? Squire thought. *Was it Brock?* He didn't remember but he remembered her. She looked different, heavier. He leaned over to whisper to Mason, "She wasn't married." They watched as she took her oath. As her hand touched the Bible, Squire thought he saw a small spark emit from its cover – enough to set off a gas leak.

"Don't worry about it," Mason replied. "Let's see how they start this thing. I like to feel the rhythm, the strategy the opposing side has and work it against them. They are about to throw down their hand and reveal their cards." Squire adjusted in his chair feeling the uncertainty of his circumstance. Was he going to have to watch himself manifested in physical form, enchanting all of his past girlfriends in this room?

"Please state your full name for the record, Miss Brock," said Woodrow P. Devine.

"My name is Paige Susan Le Monde-Brock," she replied. She looked squarely at Squire as she enunciated the hyphenated last name.

"And how do you know the defendant?" Devine asked.

"We used to date," she replied.

"I object to this witness, Your Honor," Mason stood. "This is a suit based on the Family Unity Sustainment Act. She was not married when she dated my client."

"Mr. Devine?" the judge redirected.

"Your Honor," Woodrow P. Devine sighed, "we are calling this witness to establish a pattern of behavior. Regardless of her marital status at the time, she can attest to the behavior and character of Mr. McDermott."

"I will allow it, overruled," Judge Perkins said as the gavel smashed down on the sound block.

Mason looked at Squire remembering the pretrial discovery phase. The potential witness list was excessive. There was no way Devine could call all of them. At some point the testimony would become a broken record, turning around and around playing the same broken part of a tragic song. No judge would allow it. Mason had given up trying to investigate them all. Devine's strategy to overwhelm him with an exhaustive list wasn't going to work. He had different plans once he got the chance.

"Let's see what she has to say," he whispered to Squire.

* * *

SHE MUST HAVE SAID it 50 times, *my boyfriend*, moments before their first encounter. The word, *boyfriend*, just bounced off of him like small arms fire against a tank. He had seen her around his favorite coffee shop. Her little store shared the building. It was during a time he was engrossed in discovering and studying the nature of his being.

What made him the way he was? Unidentified childhood trauma? A need for love he could not seem to grasp? What was it about his romantic journey? So many girls and almost the same goal every time. It was rare that he didn't feel something profound for each of them. The ones he attached to eventually turned away as though they were repulsed by him – a complete off-switch once he committed. Then there were girls like Paige. Something about her kept him engaged but with her he was aloof, almost irritated by her existence. He didn't have the heart to tell her and she never shut up long enough to listen.

Boyfriend, boyfriend, boyfriend… They sat there drinking a lethal concoction of rums and fruits as she talked. Eventually there was touch; the third wheel rolled away. His hand came up to pull her close. They kissed. The intensity built. There were frantic lips and hands everywhere. He led her through the door of her shop. They fell to the floor. Weeks later, when the scabs on his knees and rug burn on her ass finally healed, they had reached an understanding.

She would talk on the phone for hours and he would listen until he told her he had to go or more frequently he would just ask her to come over for the one thing that shut her up. He remembered once, after setting down the phone to relieve his bladder, he returned to his room, picked up the phone and said, "Uh-huh," like he had heard the whole conversation. She was still talking.

He walked into the kitchen; his roommate, Bryant, looked at him, "Done finally?" he asked.

"No," Squire laughed, "she's still talking."

"You just set the phone down and walked away?"

"What else am I going to do?" Squire walked into his room to retrieve the phone. His roommate watched as he said, "Yeah," and set the phone down again. "She's still talking; no idea I haven't heard anything and she doesn't care."

"You are a fucking asshole," the roommate scowled. "I am going."

"Good," Squire replied, "she's coming over." The roommate shook his head in disgust.

"You don't even like her," he replied.

"She has her good sides," Squire grinned. How he managed to get a roommate so dedicated to his church, his ideals, and the blinders directing his way through life, Squire would never know. Resentment, that was the word that defined their relationship. Resentment from the roommate and apathy in return.

Everything Squire did with a girl or girls manufactured the same response from the roommate who held it over him in triumphant judgment. Hell awaited. The roommate was nearly engaged. His girlfriend brought banana bread and cakes by the place once in a while when only Squire was there. Her innocent tap on the door sent an earthquake up his spine. All he could think of was getting her out of there before Bryant got home from work. He didn't need the suspicion. When it was the three of them, he was unwelcome. Bryant sulked and made moralistic jabs at Squire like he was trying to provoke a reaction. Bryant only earned a laugh.

Squire could tell Bryant's girlfriend sensed everything almost as though she expected there to be a fight but Squire resisted. It would serve nothing to defend himself against a man hellbent on his own destruction – a man who would limit his life to the *shoulds* of societal norms. He convinced himself that he was better than Squire, the cheater; convinced himself because, with Bryant, even virtue was a competition. Eventually the girlfriend disappeared and the real Bryant was revealed.

But at this moment, as he sat in court, those *shoulds* seemed like the path he should have taken. They were safe. They went somewhere. They were packed down trails by those who went before him but his world was like standing in a grassy field; the only path led up behind him to where he stood. There was nothing ahead, only the flowers of prairie grass blowing in the breeze.

"Hey," he interrupted, "come over so we can really talk."

"OK," Paige replied. "You know I am not breaking up with my boyfriend…"

"Thank god."

* * *

SQUIRE WATCHED Paige shift nervously back and forth in her chair. He turned to look at the gallery. There was no one who looked like a husband there. Squire took in a deep, therapeutic breath.

"Mrs. La Monde-Brock," Woodrow P. Devine began, "tell us about your relationship with Squire McDermott."

Paige sat a little straighter. Squire felt anxious. Devine had opened a box that may never shut. "Well, he used to hang out at this coffee shop near my boutique. I know him from there. Then he asked me out and I said 'No' and he kept persisting so eventually I went out with him."

"You went out with him because he kept persisting?" Devine asked.

"Yeah," she replied, "sometimes you have to just see if a guy is different on a date than when he is just hanging around you."

"Were you married at the time?" Devine asked.

"No, I was sort of seeing someone. It wasn't serious," she answered.

Squire squirmed. His hands clenched into fists as he listen

to the betrayal of truth before him. Mason's hand patted his forearm, reassuring him. "We'll get our turn," he whispered.

* * *

Squire thought back to their purely sexual relationship. There was something about her he couldn't commit to. She was cute, sort of like a spinner. If he had a weakness, it was spinners. All of his sapiosexual preferences evaporated when the woman was tiny, easy to carry around. If he had a kink, spinners were the living embodiment of it. He knew it was pure fetish. Paige certainly didn't look like one now. He found himself grasping for a memory of what she was like. Scenes of their escapades coursed through his mind. After the first encounter, they had evolved into friends. The physical connection was gone. Then the dog sitting episode...

She met him out on the street as he walked his friend's malamute. Outside the dog was fine, inside was another reality. She had lost her puppies a week before and was taking it out on the world from under the guest bed – random episodes of gnashing teeth every time he turned over. How he had gotten himself involved in watching the dog he would never remember but he did it.

Paige was really flirty with him that night as they walked. Her little body was alive, she was pensive as if she was up to something. It had been over a year since the hook up. The flame was out and Squire had no expectations for anything but friendship. She told him she was coming over to see the dog then she would go home, nothing more. It was done. They were done. His roommate's moralism had been vindicated.

He invited her in for one last furry pet of the bottled up rage before it retreated under the bed to sulk and snarl. Paige sat down on the couch looking like she had no intentions of leaving. "Would you like a glass of wine?" He asked. She nodded.

The glasses pinged against each other as they chatted around the inevitable. With an intention he had never seen in her, her wine glass planted itself upon the coffee table; she slipped down between his knees. He gave her minutes to fulfill this most obvious seduction before he pulled her shirt over her head and picked her up. As she straddled him, he carried her towards the monster living below. With a feat of strength, he heaved himself and Paige over the gnashing teeth to the safety of an awaiting mattress. As Squire and Paige rolled in ecstasy, pummeling each other with pleasure the dog howled out in anguish for her puppies. There came a moment he couldn't tell the difference between the screams of Paige and the howling, "Oh my God, whoooo, Jesus, fuck, whooo, whooooooo, grrrrr!" But he forged on until both had succumbed.

The morning came, he felt her next to him fast asleep. Serene. Her fur glistening in a sunbeam through the window. Paige was gone.

* * *

"Would you classify Mr. McDermott as a cad, a player?" Woodrow P. Devine asked.

"Objection, leading," Mason spoke up.

"Sustained," Judge Perkins groaned. "Rephrase your question, Mr. Devine."

"In your own words," Devine continued, "how would you describe Mr. McDermott?"

"He's a player," Paige sputtered. "He knew I had a boyfriend and he still pursued me."

"How long did you know him?" Devine asked.

"A few years. We were friends but there was always something weird about it."

"Can you describe what was weird?"

"You know, it's just a feeling I got. *The ick.*"

Squire shuttered, the *ick*. He had never heard a woman say that about him. It pained him deeply to be described that way. What he had with women he looked back at fondly regardless of the outcome. What was making Paige turn so abruptly against him?

They seemed to select their memories in a move towards their strategic defense. Was everything, every joy, every embrace, every orgasm just something they could deny later like nothing ever happened? Discretion had come back to haunt him. Like a cameraman who forgot to push record, the scene never happened. But he wasn't that; this was real to him.

Squire liked all of them, some of them he thought he loved. *I think maybe I am like a girl*, he thought to himself. *I bond through sexual intimacy. Do other guys do that?* Paige's testimony was a shock. She seemed to deny everything. Down to the last day he lived nearby, she had pursued him. She called him and talked and talked. She was one of the most enthusiastic women in the bed he had ever experienced. She set the bar.

But now, according to her, it never happened like that. He worried about what Mason was going to do to her. Exposing the lies seemed wrong. He couldn't allow his attorney to call her out. "Don't hurt her," he scribbled on his legal pad. "She is different now. Don't dig a hole in the past and throw her in."

Mason looked at the words in front of him. He understood.

"Mr. Braddock, your witness."

Mason stood, Paige shrunk. Squire took a deep breath hoping Mason really understood.

"Mrs. Brock, did you and the defendant ever engage in consensual sexual intercourse?"

Paige blushed, "We did."

"Do you recall which of you pursued whom?"

"He pursued me," Paige answered.

"And you relented?"

"I gave in. You know, he just kept asking so I just sort of gave in," Paige replied. She looked lost for words. Her gaze became fixed upon Devine. Mason turned to look at Woodrow who sat innocently staring up at the ceiling. She had been coached too well. Her role was to establish Squire as a predator – someone who badgered women until they gave in. He would find a weakness in her, bide his time and exploit it. Why would she do this?

"How was the sex?" Mason asked.

"Objection!" Woodrow P. Devine yelled.

"Sustained," the judge agreed.

Mason regrouped. "How many times would you say that you and Mr. McDermott engaged in intercourse?"

Her hesitation spoke for itself, "Maybe once," she replied.

"Maybe once?" Mason challenged.

"Yeah, once," Paige answered. "I really don't even remember it."

"And that was where?"

"At his place."

Squire winced. Mason stepped back towards their table to retrieve a light blue sweater. "Does this look familiar?"

"I think that was mine," she answered.

"Your Honor I would like to enter this sweater into evidence," Mason said as he handed it to the bailiff.

"Could you take a look?" he asked. "Try it on."

Paige looked over the sweater. She slipped it on. It seemed snug. "Doesn't fit," she said.

"Are you the same size now as when you had sex with my client?"

"I have gained a few pounds," she grumbled.

"How many pounds, estimated?

"Twenty?" Paige replied. "I don't know. Where did you get this? It's not mine."

Squire saw Devine's eyes widen. He looked irritated, concerned.

"Can you verify that it is not your sweater?" Mason said.

"It's not my sweater," Paige shot back.

CHAPTER 5

"Come on, we're going to get tacos," Mason coaxed Squire along. "There's a good place across the street. Great tacos, non-gentrified, auténticos, sin influencia gringosa." There were three tables taken of the twenty. Mason slid into a booth gesturing to Squire. "Trust me, this place is awesomo."

"That's not Spanish," Squire laughed.

"How many Latinas do you think are going to throw you under the autobús?" Mason paused waiting for Squire to respond before he continued, "I can't wait to hear Victoria's bullshit." Squire seemed to tense up.

"You think she'll be called?" Squire asked.

"If Woodrow knows what he is doing, he won't call her. I'll roast that chick."

"Oh man, don't do that," Squire groaned. "She was great. I suffered when we split. It was like we were meant for each other, soulmates or something. We connected on too many levels." Squire's memory flowed off into the ether. "Chemistry...," he sighed.

The waitress approached. She was young, early twenties

maybe. Mason watched as Squire's eyes met hers. She smiled. Her posture shut out Mason. It was obvious there was something in Squire she liked. Although she could have pivoted a foot and landed on Mason's lap, she had positioned herself fully for Squire's attention. Mason looked up at her and barked out the order. She spun towards the kitchen.

He had no idea what came over him. It seemed like jealousy, maybe more like envy. He was an accomplished lawyer sitting across from a somewhat disheveled man who looked out of place in a suit and the waitress completely ignored him. It was incredible that she would fixate like that on Squire.

What was it about this guy and women? What was it about his own reaction? It seemed to degrade almost automatically to willful combat. As Mason looked up at Squire, he realized that the girl hadn't fazed him at all. There was no projection of lust or need. He just smiled at her with no intentions, desire-less. And it was not a façade he was putting up.

Then it struck him; it was safe. Squire was the safest, most naturally sexual being Mason had ever met. And he was on the edge of being clueless about it. He had no idea what attracted women to him. Is that what the women were responding to? It had to be. That's why they wanted him. That's why their morals, their ethics, and their oaths were so urgently tossed aside. It was almost as though they had to take a little taste of that piece of chocolate in the middle of a diet. He was guilty pleasure. Mason began to think that the trial might devolve into damage control in place of triumph. But it wasn't time to panic, not yet. They were three hours into a trial that could go all week. It could go a month and Squire seemed to have no money.

* * *

"ALL RISE," the bailiff commanded, "the Honorable Judge Montague S. Perkins presiding." They rose as the judge entered. As Squire sat down he looked back towards the gallery, there were notepads in front of people who looked like reporters. Feeling an urge to shrink, he slouched in his chair until Mason tapped him back upright.

"Call your next witness," the judge said.

"Your Honor, I call Miss Brianna Duncan as our next witness," Woodrow P. Devine announced.

"She's still alive," Squire whispered with relief as Brianna strolled in, "thank God." Mason looked at him wondering what he had meant. The Bible was presented again. Brianna took her oath – no flash of light, no spark.

"Miss Duncan," Devine began, "it is *Miss*, correct?"

"Yes, I am single," she confirmed.

"Do you have children?"

"I have two."

Squire perked up. Two. She had one when they were together.

"It must be hard to manage with a career," Devine said as he tugged at his belt.

"It is," she replied. She looked directly at Squire, "I realize now that everything would have been easier if we could have worked it out."

"Between you and the father?" Devine asked. Mason was about to protest. Where was this going? Was this chitchat really necessary? Was it pertinent? He took a deep breath and tried to relax.

"The fathers..." she corrected. "They have different fathers."

Devine seemed to squirm. Mason had experienced his well-coached witnesses before. This one might be more than Woodrow expected now that she had an audience.

"Please tell the court how you and Mr. McDermott met."

***

He didn't know what came over him. Every time he looked up she just stood there, pleading for him without words as he wiped down the bar. Her friends kept tugging at her; she was their responsibility for the night.

"Did you win the pageant?" he winked.

Her tiara was half-cocked on her head, her sash glittered through hints of spilled margaritas. *Bride*, it said. Her cute little mouth turned upward.

"When's the wedding?" Squire asked.

"Two weeks," she said.

"Congratulations."

"Yeah."

"You OK?" he asked. Tears came to her eyes. The look on her face hit him. Something protective in him came to life as he slid his phone to her. "If you want to talk to someone neutral..."

She grabbed the phone and pounded her number into the keypad as her friends seemed to materialize from every direction, tugging her away from the bar. Brianna was able to throw the phone back at Squire who caught it just before it crashed through the rack of bottles behind. One of her friends stood in front of him, hands on hips, scowling like she was ready to tackle him if he pursued. There would be none of that sort of thing on her watch. As they dragged Brianna out, she cast one last longing look at him.

The shift was long, outside of his normal Happy Hour routine, but he had made a lot of money. Men circled the bachelorette parties buying drinks, making sure their tips were noticed.

His phone vibrated the nightstand, *Wanna talk?*
Yeah, you OK? You seemed a little upset.
I'm OK

Then the dam broke. She poured out her heart to him rationalizing her wedding, the man. He was a mechanical engineer. He had his own house. They had been dating for almost a year. She was a single mother. She needed this sort of stability in her life. She was closing in on thirty. She looked younger to Squire. He told her. She responded with a red lip emoji.

Squire shuddered, red lips. *Oh no*, he thought.

She went on talking about her experience with men, especially the father of her daughter. Squire remained neutral. It wasn't like him to openly discredit a man he didn't know or any man for that matter. When a woman wanted him, he followed her lead, her desire, her wants. They pursued him. For most of his life he had nothing to offer but himself and they seemed happy with that for a while. *For a while*, was the thing that plagued him.

Eventually they would realize that he wasn't two opposing types of men conjoined into one. This was Brianna. The words changed, the questions became more future oriented, more serious, and foretelling. What were his life goals? Where did he see himself in five years? The underlying, never spoken, part of the question was: how will I benefit from you? What am I going to get out of this?

Squire didn't know the answer. His life was lived as the sun rose and set. He had money saved but not due to expectation or anxiety. He didn't think to spend the extra on much more than a dinner out once in a while with a woman he liked. He drove an old pickup truck when he drove at all. With women, it never mattered. At first they thought it was fun, it aroused something in them.

Somehow Brianna's wedding was postponed. The groom agreed. She needed to work some things out. Those things were Squire.

"When did you first begin dating Mr. McDermott?"

Woodrow P. Devine huffed as he forced his frame up off his chair in a feat of pendular momentum.

"It was right after we met," Brianna sighed. "When my wedding was postponed..." Mason snatched up his pen to scribble a note.

Devine halted. This line of questioning could go wrong. "In your words, tell the court about the courtship between you and Mr. McDermott."

Brianna let out a little laugh and paused, struggling for the right words. "Courtship," she sighed. "We...um... It was very physical." The judge tapped the sound block and scanned the gallery as laughter subsided. Squire felt for Brianna. She looked miserable. He wondered why she was there. Why she had submitted herself to this?

"No dates? Dinners? Movies?" Devine asked. "No drives in the countryside? Picnics?"

"We watched movies in bed," she interrupted.

Devine glared at her. Her answers were to come when he looked at her, after a pause like she was coached. He hesitated wondering if he should just drop the questioning now and avoid any more potential fodder for Mason Braddock. Under the amiable charm he projected towards everyone, he hated Mason. Woodrow knew why he took this case. Mason was defending himself as much as he was defending McDermott. He remembered Mason's outburst when the Family Unity Sustainment Act passed almost unanimously.

"The reason this passed is because you chumps think your wallets and servitude has sustaining sexual value," he had shouted. "None of you has ever attracted a woman with anything but that and you never will. Your virtue is based in provisioning until death and you all serve a false god shaped like a giant, golden vagina! Fuck you, fuck this law and fuck democracy! I take that last part back. But fuck all of you twice!"

It was the most childish, repulsive rant Woodrow P. Devine had ever heard from another attorney.

* * *

"Squire, oh my god," she screamed as her forehead bounced on the drum head. The rhythm was haunting, resonant, and tribal. Boom, boom, boom, boom, boom…He had built it as a joke in a community woodworking cooperative. It was exquisite, a light, natural, clouded maple with cherry highlights. A massive 40-inch concert bass drum head was set into the headboard, stretched timpani style and tuned to a frequency an internet guru had suggested to be the most erotic and enchanting.

The drum glowed in faint lavender. She had chosen the color for the night. Months and months since they met and they were *making up* again. It was the same problem every time. The same problem for her. As much as Squire aroused her, he just wouldn't change and become the man she thought he could be. She pushed and he retracted and she chased him down. The cycle was on repeat.

"You're so smart and talented," she sighed as she nestled in close to him. "Didn't you ever want to do more with your life?"

Squire remained quiet. Anything he said would be in defense of who he was. It felt wrong to be on edge like this. He liked who he was. Behind the bar he was an artist; in his soul he was an artist. Everything that interested him was an art form that fed who he was and how he saw the world. To chase money behind an excuse of art was, to Squire, the highest form of demonic self-absorption. He left that all to the power thirsty, the others who would seek their ends no matter the means.

He was his own means to incomprehensible ends. He flew

forward feeling the wind push him along against his wings. She perceived an outcome for him. One created in her mind and in her hopes – an outcome that involved who they were together at that moment combined with a sense of security she had never felt. The more she reached for it, the further she pushed it away. Brianna would never be content.

* * *

"He broke up with me and told me I should get back with my fiancée," a tear ran down her cheek. "For a long time I thought we had something. I was wrong. Then I realized that I had almost lost the real man I deserved. Squire did me a favor but he made me feel used."

"Mr. Braddock, your witness."

Mason stood, "Hello Miss Duncan, would you say that you hoped my client would have been a better provider for you and your children? Someone to step into the role and responsibilities of another man?"

"Objection!" Woodrow P. Devin bellowed. "He is leading the witness."

"Overruled," the judge said. Devine looked shocked. He called for a sidebar.

Squire watched as Devine complained. Mason stood back, hands crossed waiting for the judge's opinion. Devine's shoulders crumpled. Mason gave Squire a devilish grin as he stepped back to the lectern.

"You may answer the question, Miss Duncan," Judge Perkins instructed.

"Um, I guess so," she sighed. "I wanted him to use his talents more. He had so much potential."

"Can you describe what your expectations were for him?" Mason asked. Woodrow growled, attracting the judge's scornful gaze.

"You know, to be *more*," she repeated.

Mason took a deep breath. He was going to have to answer for her. "You wanted more income? More dependability? More confidence in the future? More prestige? More like other men?"

"Objection," Woodrow grumbled. "The last statement about other men, Your Honor."

"Sustained, the jury will disregard the statement about other men."

"Would you say that my client attracted you initially because he was different?"

"Yes," he replied.

"What was your late husband like?" Mason asked.

"Objection! Late husband, indeed. This is irrelevant!" Woodrow screamed.

"Your Honor, the question is relevant in establishing my client as an outlier to society, someone outside the expected norms who, for whatever reason, naturally attracts women. In no way is the natural impulse of his behavior illegal. Is has been made illegal by an unjust law imposed by unattractive men – men who eventually self-implode such as Miss Duncan's late husband."

"Mr. Braddock! You are out of order. There will be no more outbursts like this!" The gavel slammed down.

CHAPTER 6

"Just go. I'll deal with them," Mason said as they walked out into the swarm. Squire was overwhelmed by the sight.

"Squire! Where is Squire McDermott?" a thirty-something, blond reporter yelled. Squire hesitated. Mason's hand planted squarely on his back shoving him away towards the parking garage.

"I'll take a few questions. My client is off limits for now," Mason said as he stepped into the fray.

"What do you hope to accomplish by this?" a man asked as he pushed a microphone towards Mason.

"Vindication for a man whose reputation is being lynched in the name of an emotionalized and unjust law."

"It is obvious that he had sex with those women," the reporter rebutted. "How many more?"

"Are you implying that consensual sex between adults is retroactive victimhood when the results of that sex become one of the willing participant's marital problems or the fuel of a guilty conscience?"

"Under the law," the reporter replied smugly, "he has a duty to verify the status of the woman."

"Hold on there, mister," Mason laughed. "The law wasn't written only for men. All parties have the duty under the law to verify marital status. What about disclosure? When does that happen? The problem with this law is that it has become the default assumption that the law is to protect women from being victimized by their own innate desires. This law was made by men for men. It is a legalized attempt at mate-guarding by men lucky enough to have convinced a woman to marry them by whatever means they were capable. This is a law based in virtue at the expense of nature. It is a law that criminalizes my client for the sexual arousal he elicits in women based solely on who he is. It seems virtuous the way men like you have constructed this law.

"It's a feeble attempt at religiosity in an irreligious culture. Unjust and antiquated moralistic thinking created it. It is an attempt at forcing your virtues onto others in a legally binding framework ignoring the reality that sometimes people just want to fuck. That includes women." The cameraman's mouth went agape.

"So when you are with your wife because you got a bonus or behaved well and she gives it up to keep to you on the hook, know this: she's just not that enthusiastic about it. She's just doing it because she's used to it, it doesn't take long, and she can get back to dreaming about real desire." With that, Mason turned on his heels and stomped off laughing. He had just laid bare the realities between the average man and Squire. Now they had bigger problems.

*　*　*

THEY SAT in Squire's apartment watching the edited version. "The law wasn't written only for men...," Mason retorted then the shot cut away as if it were looking for Squire in the crowd.

"I think they really wanted to talk to you," Mason observed. "Obviously, that's impossible for most of them."

Squire agreed with a nod, "You didn't talk to the blond?"

"No, why?" Mason hesitated. "God, don't tell me." The look on Squire's face revealed everything. "What? When?"

"A couple of year's ago, did you see the rings?" Squire asked. "She didn't have those then," Squire said.

"What's your count, Squire?"

"I don't understand."

"Your lay count? How many women?" Mason asked, wondering how many more potential problems they might have.

"I don't know," Squire answered sheepishly. "I mean I lost track in my twenties when I was a bartender in the Caribbean and Mexico. And I was a ski instructor… It seems like the only time I was not getting laid is when I had a steady girlfriend or I tried to hide." He tried to laugh.

"And how often was that?"

"Almost never," Squire sighed.

"Why? I mean, I know why, but why?" Mason asked.

"I don't know," Squire replied. He looked like his frustration was ready to well up. The question hit on something deeply internal.

"I know why," Mason said. "You are still chasing something you think is missing."

"What?"

"A poetic ideal of love you *wish* were true…"

* * *

"All rise…"

Mason looked at Squire. He looked like he hadn't slept.

He looked worn down, thrown into a self-dug pit to rot for his misdeeds.

"Your Honor, I call Mr. Howard Alistair Cullen to the stand," Woodrow P. Devine announced. He seemed proud today, confident.

Mason nudged Squire pointing out the scribble on his pad *Howard Alistair Cullen, HACk*, hoping his client would ease up on himself. The trial was becoming an unintended journey of self-discovery into the pits of Squire's imagined hell.

Howard Cullen began with his courtship of Victoria, "I met her at a country club party. At the time, she was not a member. I was stunned by her beauty and told her."

"Do you remember what you said?" Devine asked.

Howard recalled the words, "Yes, I told her I thought she was the most beautiful women in the world."

"Sounds like a wonderful beginning to a wonderful relationship," Devine gushed. Mason groaned. The comment had obviously been to tug at the jury's heartstrings. He looked over at Squire who sat blank-faced listening. But the comment seemed to resonate with him.

"Sadly, Victoria is feeling like she should avoid the country club since all this started and I have added at least ten strokes to my golf game," Howard sighed, looking out at the gallery for sympathy. What had been a haven for them, a demonstration of their place in society, had turned into a gossip-generating cauldron of vile banter. There was always at least one target of gossip at the club and now it was them.

Mason looked like he wasn't paying attention. He stared at the ceiling, seemingly unaware and uncaring. Squire glanced at Victoria, she stayed rigidly focused ahead like someone in a neck collar. He had heard all the stories. She was going to leave Howard. Every orgasm strengthened her resolve to give up the country club for the topsy turvy world of being Squire's girlfriend. It excited her to go out with him to places she knew the country clubbers wouldn't go.

"Don't worry," she reassured him. "They don't go anywhere, only to the club. It's their life. It's like a sorority that only allows well-behaved men to enter. I try to take my friends out. They always feel like we are traitors so we go back and watch the same people dancing to the same band like they have over and over and over. How can gringas be so boring?"

The way she talked to him, that accent, those moves. There was something about her hips no American woman could begin to learn. She lamented about Howard, how sterile he was in bed except for his fetishes, his kinks. For whatever reason, he really like to have a vibrating butt plug in him but he would never give her the remote control. He did it himself. She thought his control freakishness about it was more odd than the plug. Why not let her drive once in a while?

How could he be so sterile and so kinked out? Squire asked himself as he watched the man try to conjure tears over his struggling marriage. He drew a picture of a butt plug and slid it to Mason then drew an arrow straight at Howard. Mason's face contorted attempting to suppress his laughter.

Not surprised, he wrote on the pad. *Someone should stick one in his mouth.* Squire and Mason both laughed out loud just as Howard was speaking of his mother and the pain the trial was causing her. The gavel slammed down five times; the room hushed.

Judge Perkins glared at them. "Proceed," he finally said to Woodrow P. Devine.

It was nearly impossible for Mason and Squire to remain calm. Once an inside joke was uncaged, it took over their consciences. The gavel pounded again, "We'll take a 15-minute break. Counsel, see me in my chambers."

"Stay here unless you have to piss or something," Mason advised. Squire froze.

Howard Cullen sat down next to his wife, she spun in her chair to face him. As he leaned in to whisper something, Victoria looked past him directly at Squire. The eyes teared, she mouthed, "Lo siento, mi amor," and kissed the air. Squire sat nearly comatose. She hadn't forgotten him.

For Victoria, Squire was what Mason had described to him the night before; he was the ghost haunting her emotions. He was the man every back-up plan chump knows lives somewhere in his wife. The one who just got it and gave it to her. Sometimes that man was make-believe, conjured into her fantasies: a famous actor, a sports hero, a musician but for the chumps who were bound to suffer for a lifetime, the ghost was real. No amount of expensive cars, dinners, or vacations could erase what the ghost put inside her.

Mason walked out of the judge's chambers looking like an incorrigible school boy who had just lied to the headmaster about correcting his behavior. He sat down next to Squire, his face emotionless.

"Mr. Braddock, your witness."

"Mr. Cullen," he began, "you have been married how long?"

"Twenty-three years and counting," Howard quipped.

Mason paused, he shuffled through his notes. "How's your sex life?" He turned towards Devine expecting an objection. All was quiet at the opposing table. Victoria looked anxious.

"In what way?" Howard asked.

"In every way, Mr. Cullen. Are you kinky?"

"Objection!" There it was, what Mason was hoping for.

"Approach," the judge ordered.

"Mr Braddock, where is this going?" Judge Perkins asked.

"Your Honor, I am establishing the nature of a sex life in a normal, upper-class, White Anglo-Saxon Protestant household. Does it mesh with the norm?"

"What is the norm?" the judge asked.

"Coitus periodicus normalus," Mason replied.

"Don't make up words," Devine sputtered, "Judge? He's…"

Judge Perkins held up his hand quieting Woodrow, "I am guessing that this is part of your overall strategy? Is that right, Mr. Braddock?"

"Yes, Your Honor," Mason replied.

"Proceed, but choose your words…" Judge Perkins instructed.

"Mr Cullen, allow me to ask a different way," Mason smiled as he looked up from his notes. "Are you happy with your sex life with Mrs. Cullen?"

"I am," Howard sat up a little straighter.

"Is she?"

"I am not sure what you mean by the question," Howard shot back.

"Does she have orgasms, Mr. Cullen?"

"Of course she does!"

"How do you know?" Mason asked.

"She tells me," Howard grumbled. "How else would I know?"

"Spasms, uncontrollable muscular spasms in the pelvis, buttocks, the legs is one way," Mason grinned. "Have you ever seen that? Have you seen involuntary muscle contractions? Heavy breathing that seems out of this world? Flushed skin? Serious and uncontrollable moaning?"

"Objection!"

"Overruled!" The gavel pounding was serious. The judge threatened to remove the gallery who looked like they were about to explode.

Mason let the courtroom's collective libido and excitement subside as he shuffled his notes again.

"Mr. Cullen," Mason was deadpan serious, "do you insert mechanical stimuli into your anus to heighten your sense of pleasure?"

Howard Cullen looked as if he was about to jump across the room and pound Mason to death. The gallery was completely out of control. Judge Perkins stood, pounded the gavel again and motioned for another sidebar.

"I will hold you in contempt if you pull that shit again," Judge Perkins growled. "What are you establishing?"

"Sexual satisfaction is all about him," Mason replied innocently.

"Shut up, Woodrow," the judge interjected as Devine began to open his mouth. "I don't need your opinion on this. And you, Mr. Braddock, get past the kinky shit and start making sense."

"Mr. Cullen, when you confronted Mrs. Cullen," Mason went on, "did she describe the sex she allegedly had with my client."

"She did," Howard replied.

"Was there anything out of the ordinary? Any kinks?" Mason asked.

"Nothing like that... I didn't really ask and she didn't give me too much information. Just that they had sex a few times," Howard stumbled.

"How many is a few times?" Mason asked.

"I don't know," Howard was becoming uncomfortable.

"Did you ask her for details regarding the act of sex with my client?"

"I think so."

"It is common for men to want in on the details, Mr. Cullen. It fuels their anger and indignation," Mason challenged. "Did you or did you not ask?"

'I did!" Howard spouted back.

"Please describe for the court what she told you," Mason replied, attempting to suppress a grin.

Howard Cullen hesitated. His eyes began to water as he thought back to that day after the dentist when he confronted her. He kept probing, asking and asking about what she meant until she finally confessed to the affair. Then, in his rage, he pushed harder. What had she done? He remembered using the word anal. Had she done that? Oral? How much oral? Did he do oral on her? He wanted a list. He could not believe that some poor bartender had been able to satisfy his wife with such benign sounding sex. She had to be lying. Everyone of his friends at the country club alluded to their kinks, the kinks of their wives, paying for kinks with escorts. Kinks were a way of life.

What made Squire Fucking McDermott so special that he could get her off in missionary position and whatever the hell borboleta paraguaia was? Was that even Spanish? In her distress, she kept saying borboleta paraguaia and frango asado like he should understand. He looked them up on the internet. It was Portuguese. Was she fucking a Brazilian too? He started keeping a close eye on her, enlisting friends from the club to assist. Then the marriage counseling. It seemed to work. She got back into line.

In the end, he would do anything to keep her. Somehow her affair cost him thousands of dollars but they were whole again. She was receptive to his touch. She looked at him like she had on their first official date at whatever that restaurant was called. Through glasses of French wine and filet mignon he watched her fall in love. She made him wait for sex. Every woman had made him wait. It was innocent. It was moral and virtuous. He wondered how long she had made Squire McDermott wait but couldn't get himself to ask. It didn't matter, she was his and she would stay that way.

"One last question, Mr. Cullen," Mason looked up from

his notes. "Did Mrs. Cullen inform you that she did not tell Mr. McDermott that she was married?"

"What does it matter?" Howard shot back. "She has a ring."

"What if she wasn't wearing it?"

Howard Cullen rolled his eyes, "She has a permanent tan line on her ring finger."

CHAPTER 7

Squire slid Mason's gin and tonic towards him and recentered himself behind the bar. The customers lingering around were mixed; they all had seen the news footage. Some came in for support but most came in to look for Squire McDermott in the place he supposedly worked.

A handsome older man seated near Mason excused himself to go to the restroom. Mason had been watching the couple. The woman was smitten with Squire and was acting a little inebriated. With her husband out of the way, she stretched over the bar and grabbed Squire by the belt pulling him closer. Mason watched the interchange.

Squire remained calm, unfazed. She looked up at him and stumbled out some words to which Squire laughed, responding before she tripped off to the restroom. Mason hesitated; had he heard what he thought he heard?

"She just said to you, 'If I weren't married, I would fuck your brains out,'" Mason muttered somewhat in shock. He was trying to remember if he had ever seen a come-on so blatant.

"Yeah, that's what she said," Squire laughed.

"When a married woman says that, do you think 'you have my number' is the wise response?"

"Look," Squire replied, "I am not going to sleep with her. She has been subtly after me for a long time. If I had wanted to, I could have gotten with her a couple years ago. She lives in my neighborhood. Her husband seems like a cool guy. What I did was horn her up for *him*. She is going to take that sexual energy home right now and fuck *his* brains out."

"Thinking about you," Mason challenged.

"Maybe, but he won't know and he won't care," Squire replied. "It will be like the wind blew just right and he did just the right things and she fucked him rotten. He'll try to think about the moves he made and repeat them. Who knows, maybe it will work again."

"You're saying you were helping him on purpose, like a wingman?" Mason asked.

Squire stopped to think about the question. "Yes, like that," he grinned, "like a guy with wings."

"You know, he probably hates you deep down," Mason said.

Squire sighed. It was a burden he carried within him for years – the silent contempt he felt from men who had neither seen who he really was nor talked to him but found a way to hate him nonetheless. Now as he looked out over the crowd, he could sense it. One-on-one with men was dramatically different than a group. With Mason, he could talk about women. Mason was someone who would be engaged and attend to a conversation.

He remembered talks with other men – how they projected subtle excitement when they asked him about his exploits and he reluctantly responded. How they projected envy without so many words. Then they would make attempts to match stories of their conquests – lies like hardened shells protecting their egos. Everything eventually devolved to competition.

But the same singular man, added to a group, would almost always gang up with the others to shame him. He was the player and they were nice guys. He was a misogynist and they respected women. There was strength in their numbers – strength in their indignant jabs, virtue signaling, and the especially the strength of their lies.

A group of relatively inexperienced men was like a colossus, the conglomeration of many melded together to form one mind. Mix a woman into the group and their morality intensified. She may say nothing but they would speak for her as though she needed them to defend her against him. Squire often wondered if men could be themselves without the overly excited clown performance so many of them fell back on when a woman was within earshot.

Squire thought about Mason's comment again. *He probably does hate me,* he thought. "I think he is suspicious," he replied.

"Rightfully so."

"Because of me? Or because of his wife? Remember, 'two to tango,'" Squire said. "Walk with me on the beach some time and I'll show you how secure men are with their women."

"How do you mean?"

"I see it all the time, the subtle reach for her hand when another man who makes him feel insecure about himself approaches. The little touches to remind her he's there. The quick invention of conversation… I see it. Is it protection or is it possession? Is it something else? Fear? It's too consistent to be something I want to see."

"Are you sure about that?" Mason asked. "Are you sure it's not an excuse for your overly experienced reality?"

Squire suddenly looked up towards the door, "Uh-oh."

Mason turned to look. One of the reporters was coming right towards them. "Oh shit," Mason growled.

"Hello," she said with a toss of her hair as she invited herself into the conversation. "You two hang out? I thought lawyers were more professional than to socialize with their clients in bars."

"We're nearly as professional as journalists," Mason grunted as he slid away towards the restroom, casting a warning glare at Squire before rounding the corner.

"Squire McDermott," she said, "can you make me a martini?"

"Dirty?" he asked.

She did this little thing with her mouth, a partial look of surprise, a little bit of tsk that came out as a punctuated *uh*. He stared down into her eyes. Hazel. They were hazel. He felt like he couldn't move; he was entranced. She just sat there, her eyes dancing back and forth into his. She made the smallest bite to her lower lip. He took a deep breath. His eyes were drawn to her lips then back trying to focus in on something. He didn't know what. Her head tipped a little to the left or maybe the right. He couldn't tell which direction was up or down or where. His fingers tingled. His whole body was lost in her. His consciousness became a distant island: offshore, uninhabited, mysterious.

"The dirtiest," she whispered.

Mason walked up, took his coat off his stool, took a look at the shimmering wall of heat between Squire and the reporter and walked out.

* * *

"FUCKING HOPELESS," Mason scolded him. "The reporter.

Literally everyone knows who she is. Every guy in this town wants her. How? You just met her."

"I am famous now," Squire grinned.

"Infamous," Mason corrected.

"I think that might be the same thing."

"That's called dark triad," Mason added. "Bad boy power, bad boy syndrome. It's different than fame."

"I don't think it's a syndrome," Squire countered.

"Whatever it is, please try to put a lid on it for a while," Mason complained. Squire laughed. Nothing could take away from his supposed triumph of Monica Beaumont, local news reporter/ Instagram model. He wanted Mason to keep believing he had slept with her. Mason tapped his pen on the table as they waited for the session to start. He looked pensive, out of focus. "You understand what it is, right?"

"Sometimes I do. Take Monica, I know I would be temporary for her. I have experienced that too much to not get it by now."

"Get what?" Mason asked. He knew the answer, he wanted to hear it from Squire. He wanted some confirmation that Squire had some self-awareness.

"She's out of my league," Squire answered.

Mason's head dropped. Squire didn't get it at all. He wondered if he should tell him. Would it matter if he knew? "She's not out of your league. She just has a lot of opportunities and as she knows it. Eventually, Squire, when you aren't novel, when the infamy wears off and the spotlight goes away, she'll feel like she had caught you and she will find something else to chase.

"Leagues are up there, something to strive for. They work with the male idea of performance. *If I could just put in the effort...* That sort of thing. They create an artificial hierarchy of effort giving men internal scapegoats when they don't obtain a level they assume they deserve. Like every fat-assed chump with a lot of money who lands a model. It's in his league. Men think it's what they have to do to get a model or any woman for that matter. Total bullshit!

"She will be unobtainable to you, Squire, because you are not the opportunity she invests her looks into. Behind the eyes of every woman like that is a soul drained of substance. Or worse, a control freak who uses her looks as a source of power. Thinking in leagues is thinking in tiers of success. It negates the fact that we are all just humans trying to survive from birth to death. Some of us are so wrapped up in envy we can't live at all. We are just empty sacks of carbon. But for Monica, right now you are an impulse," Mason exhaled.

"I know," Squire laughed.

"Why are you laughing?" Mason asked.

"She is a terrible lay," he stopped to look at Mason's reaction. "She was seriously horrible," he went on, "and I didn't sleep with her. I am just assuming she is."

"Ugh," Mason sighed. "Wait, What? Why not?"

"All rise...," the bailiff interrupted.

Mason couldn't get her image out of his head as he stood for the judge's entrance. That gorgeous, little Monica – those beautiful breasts, that ass, all for nothing. Maybe he should put in the effort to get her. He cringed at the thought. He cringed at the whirlwind of images coursing through his mind, how inexpressibly awkward they seemed.

The minutes ticked by; Mason's head spun as the court came into session in front of him. Squire nudged him as Stephen Rogers took the stand.

"Mr. Rogers, how do you know the defendant?" Woodrow P. Devine looked cocky, ready for anything today. The last session had irritated him. But today, Mason Braddock Esquire had it coming.

"I have never formally met the man," Rogers said. "But he is the reason I am getting divorced."

"Divorced?" Devine replied.

"Yes, we discussed it over the weekend. Meagan and I have decided to end our marriage and it's Squire McDermott's fault!" Stephen Rogers yelled as he stood to shake his fist.

"Order!" Judge Perkins yelled. Leaning towards Rogers, "There are no outbursts like that in my courtroom. If you want to continue, you will keep your emotions in check."

Stephen Rogers nodded sheepishly but he couldn't keep his hatred for Squire from broadcasting throughout the room. The whole gallery could sense it. Monica Beaumont scribbled furiously in her notebook. There was something she didn't understand about Squire. He didn't really do it for her and she had no idea why. But as she sat listening to the testimony, he kept haunting her.

There was something. The other women had to know something – something she wanted to discover. The zipper on the sweater she wore the night before kept giving in to gravity every time he stood in front of her. It nudged its way downward towards her waist revealing more and more cleavage but he kept looking at her eyes like he was immune to breasts. She felt like there was something contrived about it but it wasn't enough to stop.

She had him the moment she walked into the bar. She knew how long he worked. Her reconnaissance had been nearly perfect. She would get one drink towards the end of his shift then invite herself to his apartment. No man could resist such a ploy. She had to see for herself what it was.

She sat waiting for him to come out of the kitchen. She waited. Another bartender stepped up in front of her asking what she would like. She remembered saying, "Squire." The bartender stood patiently in front of her.

"Uh, he's not here," she remembered him saying as a fog rolled in around her. She would have to give it another shot.

* * *

"Who's hittin' that?" a young man in a dark suit spit into the air.

"Excuse me?" Squire's response went unnoticed.

"Seriously, who's hittin' that?" he repeated as he contorted himself to leer towards the end of the bar.

Squire's head turned slowly in the direction. She was focused on her phone. Something about the young man's words disturbed him. It was either the *hittin'* or the *that*. Neither sat well with him.

"Not me," he replied in an impatient tone. "I'm not *hittin' that*, as you put it."

"Why does she keep looking over here?" he muttered. "I'm gonna hit that."

Squire wondered how brave this young man would be if Monica could hear him. He waved her over.

"Hi, Monica," he smirked, "this fine gentlemen would like to buy you a drink."

She slid onto the barstool next to him. Propping her chin up on her hands, she fell deeply into the young man's eyes, "I hear you want to buy me a drink."

"Who said that?" he stumbled. "Yeah, um sure. Yeah..."

Her eyelashes fluttered up at Squire. "Martini?" he asked. "Dirty?"

"Filthy," she giggled as she spun back towards her puzzled victim. "I am Monica Beaumont. And you?" She kept her attention on him, laughed at his awkward jokes. As Squire watched, she mastered the manipulation. The poor boy was transfixed.

With a graceful flip of her hair she handed him her phone

and called over Squire. "We need a third," she winked. "Do you want to be *le trois*?"

"Mademoiselle, you are naughty," Squire laughed. "Of course he's the *trois*. Did you get his numbers?"

"I did," she grinned.

"Then let us move this party to the boudoir," Squire exhaled. "La nuit du ménage is upon us, you little freak. Tonight we will make the essence of three wrapped into one. The moon has spoken and you are the *trois* of our ménage. I am the *un* and Mademoiselle shall be the *deux entre nous*."

"I'm, uh, I," he stuttered. He looked around for an exit.

"What's wrong?" Monica asked as her hand clenched the zipper dragging it downward. "Is it not to be? Have I been misled? There must be a mistake. Squire darling, you promised me. I need to be spanked properly. I need to be ménaged."

"It appears so, ma cherie. He is not our *trois*," Squire frowned as the young man made for the door.

"Trés bummer," Monica laughed.

Their sides hurt from laughing as he lay her on the bed. The zippered sweater lay in the corner where he had thrown it. He licked his lips as he took down at her black lace bra imagining the panties keeping it company. In a gentle, singular motion he turned her over. She let out a little expectant whimper as his hands ran up the back of her legs, over the curves of her ass. His palms stayed there cupping her; the thumbs moved slyly between her legs then backing away. Then again and again until all she could think about was him touching her. She tried to rise up to meet him, to feel him against her from behind. Her legs parted, calling him forward.

He pushed her back down as his hands moved up along her back lingering in the curvature of her waist. He wasn't about to rush this no matter how much she wanted it. His massage melted her into the bed until he began to grind himself gently against her. The bra unhooked and fell away; his hands moved around to cup and play with her breasts. She could hear his pants fall to the floor. She reached to pull up her skirt. He stopped her; spun her towards him. With a dexterity she had never experienced, her skirt and panties came off as one to join the sweater. He pulled her to the edge of the bed. Her legs wrapped around him as he pushed himself into her. His hips and her legs locked them together gyrating as if they danced the samba. He took her wrists in his hands, pinned her down as he thrust. "Oh my god, oh my god, oh Jesus!" she screamed.

It was dark outside his bedroom window. Her fingers ran around knots of his abdomen gently up over his chest, around his nipples and back back down. They both feigned sleep. Their thoughts raced wondering what the other was thinking. His hand ran up her back to the nape of her neck. He brought her lips to his...

As the sunrise lit the room, she kissed his neck. Her hand moved up between his legs. He sank into the pillow and closed his eyes as she kissed her way downward.

*** * ***

HE DROPPED HER OFF. Monica sat in her kitchen not sure what day it was. Her phone buzzed.

Are you coming in?

I think I'm sick

OK, rest up, her boss replied. She started to laugh hysterically. She would never have even thought to hold his hand, or to talk to Squire McDermott if not for the trial. He was everything she had convinced herself of what was wrong with men. All they wanted was sex: to control her, to possess her, to objectify her.

They were all such a pathetic bunch of clowns, always performing for attention. They were lies living under conveniently revealed virtues they would give up for a hint of pussy. Pathetic, disgusting pigs. But all she could think about was him, he took her and fucked her. And right now she wanted him to do it again.

CHAPTER 8

"I don't understand," Squire lamented. "She is already going cold. I don't know what to do."

Mason looked over the shoes resting on his desk at his client. They were due back in court in the morning after an unexpected break. "Just forget it," he replied. "We have a trial to deal with. You probably over-fucked her."

"What?" Squire blasted back. "What does that mean?"

Squire still wasn't getting it and Mason was out of expendable patience. It would all come out soon enough. But he did offer, "Think of it this way. You maxed out your credit card on the first date. You're like the guy who is so desperate to make a good first impression that he takes a woman out to the best restaurant in town, gets the best wine, pays for everything, and brings her a single rose. Then he sends her more flowers the next day to thank her for a wonderful evening, a hug, and maybe a peck on the cheek. He does all that after acting like a gentleman and not going full hump on her in the parking lot. Instead of doing all that, you just fucked her stupid. She got smart. You're the polar opposite of wine and dine but the results are sort of the same."

"I know she loved the sex," Squire sighed. "I didn't do any of that gentleman stuff. Should I have?"

Mason began to laugh hysterically. Through his convulsive breathing he managed to get out, "No, just give her some space. Ghost her; that should be easy for you. If she seances you back in, she's good to go. Give her the gift of dreaded distance and uncertainty. Some of them love it and they'll never admit it."

Squire knew it was worse than he made it out to be. She had said the word, *friends*. Everyone knew what that meant. He was on an implied tether. When she needed attention, she expected him to be there but as far as a long-term want, he wasn't good enough. That's how he felt, not good enough. Why was it that he could do those things with a woman, give her orgasm after orgasm and then watch her walk away like nothing happened? He commanded their sex like she asked. Unless…, maybe she wanted the command, to control the situation. Was that it? Maybe she didn't see him as controllable.

He was good enough for all the things other men craved, lusted after, and would never get from her. If he believed most men, their sexual appetites were far more complicated than his. They flexed and proclaimed the things they would do to a women as if she were a sexual stunt double standing in for the angel they presented to their parents.

Whatever it was Squire had, women seemed to surrender to him, freeing themselves of worry and complication for a while. No amount of sexual gymnastics could match that; none were necessary. But somewhere inside Monica, and in too many others, there was a woman who no longer felt the same for him, if she had felt anything.

* * *

THE GHOST OF SQUIRE MCDERMOTT

SQUIRE LEANED on the bar staring at the phone propped up by his glass. Two stools down a pretty older woman spun her stir in her drink making small talk with the bartender who was doing his best to be accommodating. He didn't hear what she said but it had been funny enough to get a little laugh. Squire's smile caught her attention. She spun the stool in his direction. He noticed her legs: thin, long, tan, and tempting.

Two men came in and sat next to her. He had seen them around. They had a tendency to hoard in on conversations especially when a single woman was nearby. The space between Squire and her remained open but now the two men took over the scene through numbers and volume along her other front. She turned away towards them; he went back to the book on his phone. He would allow the monkeys to perform their show and get out of there.

Suddenly she spun back towards him and introduced herself with a reach across the empty barstool. The way she leaned had her looking up at him. It was too intensional. Her little handshake lingered a little too long for innocence. As her eyes held his, the revelation of her cleavage was purely tactical. *Maybe this is what I need*, he thought. They shared a few laughs at stupid things together. The bartender stepped in to play referee for the two men, keeping them in the game.

Now it was the two and the bartender against one and she was in attention heaven. Squire decided to leave it up to her. "You are pretty cool, Elizabeth. I'm going to go to a bar a couple of blocks down for awhile. If you want to join me for a drink, meet me there."

"Maybe I will," she grinned.

"It has a huge bike rack out in front, you can't miss it."

Squire laughed to himself as he stepped out into the cold evening air. He felt good. "So what about Monica," he muttered. "Women still like me." He felt somewhat closer to free as he stepped into the bike rack bar. He could never remember what it was called other than the *bike rack bar*. He slipped onto a corner stool and ordered a Scotch to sip as he tried to refocus in on his reading. The whole thing about Monica was bothering him. He ricocheted back and forth between acceptance and strategies to get her back, knowing it would only push her further away. He had been through this so many times. Every time seemed like a new insult but he could feel a hint of improvement in his reaction – a hint of acceptance and it hurt a fraction less each time.

That was almost worse. The less it hurt the more he was beginning to think it was a permanent fixture of his existence. *Is love ever reciprocal?* Squire wondered. The clock spun away thirty minutes since he ordered his untouched Scotch. Squire pushed back from the bar to go to the restroom. Elizabeth wasn't coming. She had been pinned down by the bartender, under interrogation by the two men. It seemed like she clung to the attention no matter where it was coming from. But what did he know? He knew nothing about her.

He looked at himself in the restroom mirror. He saw the *tired of* look written across his face. *Time to go home*, he thought.

His thick leather soles clomped on the hardwood. The cadence of his steps declared his intent to depart. Then he stopped, she was there. His hands came to his chest to brush an assumption of dust from his shirt. He looked at the rings on his fingers, the leather bracelet. Everything seemed in order. He slid up behind her, a hand rest gently on the back of her shoulder as he sat. "Hi."

"I recognized your jacket, is this OK?"

"I can go to my left if I have to," he teased. Before he could call her over, the bartender appeared. "What would you like?"

"What's good here?" The little game between them was

on. There was something about it he couldn't resist: the push and the pull, the build and relax, the tension. This was flirting in its most refined state. It was like chasing someone who was running backwards just barely out of reach. He leaned in, brought his hand to her hair and gently brushed it back behind her ear. He held her eyes in his as he sat back. "She wants a cosmopolitan," Squire ordered for her. The bartender spun on her heals away from them. Squire could see the bartender's grey look of irritation in the bar's mirror. A little laugh escaped.

"What?" Elizabeth asked.

"I was about to leave," he answered, "and here you are."

"Those two guys were hitting on me."

"Wow, that's surprising," Squire replied with nothing more. The cosmopolitan arrived. He took it off the bar and sipped before handing it to her. His hand came up as it came to her lips. "Wait fifteen seconds. Her favorite poison takes that long," he gestured at the bartender.

"What is wrong with you?" Elizabeth laughed.

"A lot," he smiled back as his leg slipped between hers, his foot found its place on her foot rest. The move was simple, invasive. With the tiniest of shifts his knee would eventually rest innocently and deniably against the inside of her thigh. If he pressed and she responded…

* * *

"ONE OF YOU should take the stand," Woodrow P. Devine announced. Meagan and Victoria looked at each other, each hoping the other would volunteer.

"It's getting late," Stephen said as he pulled back the cuff covering his Rolex.

"Victoria will testify," Howard snapped. He had walked into the meeting full of loathing, nothing had improved since. Victoria's head snapped up, she glared at him. Howard stared straight at Devine and without a flinch, he repeated, "She will testify. And she will say whatever you want her to say. Are we done here?"

Woodrow P. Devine took a deep breath. She could be coached, she would be. He would pull the emotions out of the Latina for the jury. Her raw femininity and accent would captivate the men. It would be a fitting exclamation to the break. "How are you?" he asked Stephen.

"I am OK, the doctor says to take it easy," he replied as he put his hand on top of Meagan's.

Devine looked at them inquiringly, "You have reconciled?"

"We have," he grinned. Meagan nodded silently. A little smile forced itself out as her eyes went distantly searching for a better way to express what she was protecting. Stephen's joy was enough to envelop both of them.

"I have to admit," Woodrow P. Devine stuttered, "it's better for you to keep that to yourselves until after the trial. Your divorce is the last nail we needed through Mr. McDermott's hand. Meagan recoiled at the visual she conjured in her head of Squire suffering upon a cross. He hadn't meant harm. Her conscience was in conflict over the way the trial had come to be. Squire had connected with her in a way no other man had, giving her something she never knew existed.

He gave her a feeling of being desired so firmly and so penetrating he would live in her forever. She had asked for that. She had sought it out. But something dark and sinister inside of her had betrayed him when she was backed into the corner. She let herself be led by Stephen's vengeance.

His asphyxiating grip on her feelings of self-worth gave her nowhere to go. The marriage counselor made it seem like a good idea to stay, to fight for what they had, to give it a chance without rushing into a decision she was being told she would regret. Everything was steeped in their faith, their community, and what a Christian family is supposed to do. Against her will, she was expected to pound the last nail herself for Stephen and the children. But it was Victoria who would take up the hammer.

* * *

ELIZABETH'S HAND ran up the inside of Squire's thigh. He leaned back and watched as she teased him. He couldn't help look at her erect nipples trying to cut through her blouse. "I live right by here," she grinned. "Do you like cats?"

Without a word he dropped cash on the bar and took her hand, "Come on, it's time to show me your *cat*."

They walked out into the fresh, cool air of the evening hand in hand. She took his arm and pulled it around her as his hand slipped into the waist of her skirt pulling her closer to him. They walked as if one swaying back and forth with every step to the front door of her apartment. "How bad do you want to see my cat?" she whispered in his ear as he pulled her close. Their mouths met open, tongues playfully touched and retracted as she fumbled for her keys. "Meow," was the last word as they fell on to her bed.

Squire pushed up her blouse. His mouth massaged her stomach giving little teases as she pulled his shirt over his head. She stopped, her eyes widened. His physique was refined – broad shouldered, thousands of pushups and pull-ups had given him a vee from shoulder to waist. It was all shaved clean. Elizabeth took his nipple in her mouth running her tongue in its orbit between playful, gentle nips while his fingers slid up between her legs.

He lingered his touch where she was most expectant before running his hand back down the inside of her thigh.

As they kissed, his hand advanced and retreated playfully. He could feel a wet heat emanating through her panties but he waited. Squire hovered over her, their eyes searched each other as he ground himself against her.

Her hips forced themselves up to meet him as their thrusts against each other steadied into a union of rhythm. He pushed her bra over her breasts and took them in his mouth. Her back arched as she responded. He could feel her slipping off into another world as he sucked on her nipples. She let out a moan of a woman lost in paradise; her pelvis shook uncontrollably, her legs wrapped around him pulling him harder against her.

With a little smirk he fell on his back to her side. Her leg swung over his, her chin rested on his shoulder, her hand ran up and down from his waist to his neck, "What was that?" she whispered.

Squire stayed quiet, he wore a devilish grin as they rested. Almost an hour had passed. "Did you cum?" she asked as her hands search his pants.

"Not yet."

"God, I did."

"I know," he replied.

He thought about the situation. It was destined when she followed him to the second bar. She may as well have just said, "Let's go to my place." But that's not how the dance worked and he knew it. He wondered how other men did these things. How did they respond to such obvious attractions? He guessed they must be like him. Why wouldn't they be? He looked over at Elizabeth; she had fallen asleep. Her cat leered at him suspiciously from atop the dresser as he slipped out of bed and back into the night.

CHAPTER 9

Woodrow P. Devine stepped forward, "Mrs. Cullen, I thank you for testifying. Your bravery in this matter is exemplary." Mason could hardly contain himself. Judge Perkins scowled at the defense. It was becoming routine.

Victoria acknowledged the accolade with a timid, awkward nod uncharacteristic of her scalding hot, Colombian passions. Squire remembered how she had teased him; how she had ridden him like she was stampeding towards freedom.

* * *

"What?" she asked.

"The tan line on your finger," Squire pointed. "Are you married?"

She pulled herself off of him and fell into the sheets. Her big, brown eyes fluttered; her fingers followed the contour of his chest. Then she sat upright, her finger tips began to run up and down his body as she looked down at him. He wouldn't ask her again. She had already answered through her touch. It beckoned, *change the subject*. She was masterful. He could feel himself at the height of arousal yet again. It was a quirk of nature that made him ready so easily, so frequently.

All it took was the hint of something sexual or even beautiful. He would finish and keep going until he finished again. He would go and go until he hurt. By then his partners would have found out why they had chosen him.

It was how he was constructed. As he sat watching her on the stand he remembered how Victoria orgasmed, it was primal. Had her husband found her triggers, had he bothered to look? His mind wandered back again to the day he noticed the tan line.

Her fingertips kept running over his chest, down his stomach, down his legs, and back up to begin again. She looked at him like she was in love but never said the words. The look on her face, the touch was enough. Love was something they both knew and pursued in different directions.

Her lips found his stomach kissing her way downward to the place that could erase his memory. She held him between her breasts, stroking him as he watched. As she sedated him further she took him in her mouth. His hands clasped behind his head, her lips closed down tight on him to lecture that the tan line had no relevance and he shouldn't push the subject.

The little flurry of her tongue on him as her hand replaced her lips made his back arch uncontrollably calling her mouth back. She took his hand and placed it on her head as her mouth resumed. His strength on the back of her head, enslaved to the pumping of her hand, was what she wanted to feel.

The faster she went the harder he pumped. But she led the rhythm as if his hand was merely there for the ride letting him imagine he was in control. Something required her to satiate him – something visceral and submitting. Squire exploded in her mouth. She kept going until she had taken everything he had to give her.

Victoria dropped again to her side next to him. She drew him in, kissing him like she wanted him to share in what she had. Then the brown eyes closed, she pulled the sheets over them and held on like she never had. Squire remembered staring up at the ceiling as his thoughts finally quieted.

It was four o'clock when he awakened. She was gone. The text messages he sent went unanswered. She had slipped back behind the iron gates where she had been hidden safely away from men like him for so long.

* * *

"Mrs. Cullen, you had a brief affair with the defendant, correct?" Woodrow P. Devine asked.

"I did."

"How did you meet Mr. McDermott?"

"I was at Happy Hour with my friends at his bar after seeing *Les Mis*," Victoria recalled. "He was very charming at the time. I think I was having a life crisis; he took advantage of it and pursued me. It was a moment of weakness..."

Squire sat stunned, trying to come to terms with what she was saying. She said it so convincingly. His head spun. Was that what it was? Was that why she disappeared? Had he really just caught her at a weak point in her life? He felt sick to his stomach. She was testifying that he had been intensionally temporary, just a pill for something like a headache.

The disappearing act she had given him was one of the worst things he had ever felt. But this... The weight of his renewed sorrow lay heavy on his head pulling it downward, giving in to the shock, the despair. He couldn't look up at her any longer. He could barely hear her voice as Devine kept prodding her towards complete denial.

"You feel like he put some sort of spell on you?" Woodrow P. Devine asked.

"Objection! Leading!" Mason yelled.

"Sustained."

Woodrow paused to organize his thoughts. "Mrs. Cullen, are you aware of men called pick up artists?"

Mason's hand clenched into a fist as he waited for Victoria to answer. There wasn't much he could do now but wait for cross-examination.

"Yes, I have heard of them," she replied.

"Have you have ever met one and had that man try to seduce you?" Devine asked.

"I have," she let out reluctantly. "He's sitting over there." The finger she had so sensually run over him came up like the barrel of a gun. The whole room looked in the direction she pointed, their confused murmuring brought the gavel up and ready to pound.

Squire felt like his breath had escaped him forever as he sat comatose in despair. He glanced up; her eyes fixated on him. In them there was a loathing, pulling out whatever life-force he had left. At that moment, Squire knew nothing of goodness or love. It was all a lie. There was no love. The word was a meaningless tool in the hands of demons. His head fell into his hands. In his emptiness, he didn't have enough emotion of any kind left to shed a tear. Victoria had sucked out his soul.

"At this time I would like to show the jury the text message the defendant sent to Mrs. Cullen while she was on a flight."

Woodrow P. Devine grinned as he pulled the monitor in front of the jury angled just enough that Victoria could see it.

He dropped the transcript on the desk in front of Mason. "Is this what the defendant texted you?" he asked.

Victoria squirmed in her chair, "It is."

"Looks like pick up artistry, doesn't it?"

"Objection!" Mason yelled.

"Sustained, the jury will disregard the comment," Judge Perkins instructed. "Mr. Devine, please refrain from being so blatant."

"Your witness," Woodrow P. Devine mocked.

Mason paused to adjust his papers, giving himself enough to keep from punching Woodrow. He knew what had happened. Victoria Cullen was over-coached. Even under oath, her lies could be plausibly denied as something she felt. The strategy was to turn Squire into some sort of snake charmer whose victims were attached women tripped up at a time of emotional crisis. And there, Squire was waiting to strike.

In his occupation, there was a steady stream of the wounded limping in from the boredom of status quo luxury living. Woodrow had just called Squire a serial predator in not so many words. The woman who had pursued him had been made the pursued, the victim of trickery.

"Mrs. Cullen," Mason began, "when you pursued my client, what were your intentions?" Out of the corner of his eye he could see Devine ready to pounce.

"What do you mean?" Victoria asked innocently. "I had no intentions. I said I was having an emotional time in my life. My mother had died. He took advantage of that."

"You were close with your mother?"

"I was very close to her," Victoria answered.

"When had you seen her last?"

"It had been a few years."

Mason looked up at Victoria, "What's a few years?"

She stumbled, "I don't know. Maybe five or ten?"

"Was it five or was it ten? That seems vague for how close you were."

"Objection!" Devine shouted.

Judge Perkins leaned towards Victoria, "Please answer the questions as specifically as you can, Mrs. Cullen."

Mason waited. She stared at him. "Well?" he asked.

"It was closer to ten," Victoria replied.

Mason let out a chuckle, "No further questions, Your Honor."

* * *

WITH HIS CLIENT descending into an existential crisis, Mason thought about the end game. How could he stir up enough emotional turmoil in the minds of the jury? There was no way to know how they would decide, what their preconceptions were, nor the internal demons they all brought with them.

"We're getting there, my friend," he consoled Squire. The silent walk to Mason's office had him thinking, plotting while Squire scuffled along. For a man of his current distinction, now was not his finest moment. Something in Victoria's testimony had punctured him. At least the press, what was left of them, wasn't following along to snap pictures.

"I lost my job," Squire sighed.

"What? When?" Mason exclaimed.

"I got a text. Fired by text during the trial. When I turned my phone back on, it was there."

"They can't do that!" Mason yelled.

"They did," Squire frowned. "The owner said he didn't want the publicity of having a bartender who destroys families."

"You weren't working there then! That was a different bar."

"I know…"

"Do you have any money saved?" Mason asked.

"I have some and I have the money from when I sold my bed," Squire let out a little, hopeful laugh. "I never spent it." He wondered how the gay couple was enjoying it, if it brought joy to their home, the percussive thumping. It was almost impossible to think about it and remain in a sour mood, a wedding present for themselves after a 20-year engagement. Squire's neighbors only had to endure the bed one last time as the couple gave it a mock test run. The lady down the hall stood with a death stare for Squire, clutching her little dog, as the movers hauled it out.

Jack and Gil, he remembered their names. They were wonderful men who pounced on the chance to convince Squire to convert. When they arrived, Gil stepped in the door and paused before saying, "Oh my, you are a fine one. You call me any time you want and don't mind him," as Jack peered over Gil's shoulder to get a better look at the *bed man*. Gil's hand rested on Squire's chest, he gave Squire a look of pure, unadulterated lechery before summoning Jack forward to inspect the bed. They paid twelve thousand in cash offering twenty thousand if he would place his hands on their crotches and swear to never build another.

The happy moment back in time evaporated from his mind as he sat down in Mason's office.

"You OK?" Mason asked. "She really got to you, didn't she?"

"Yeah, I don't know why. Maybe it's not about her," Squire sulked. "It's like I just started to realized that love doesn't exist. How I think of it, anyway."

"Did she profess her love for you?"

Squire shrugged, "Not in words, but I knew she did. Then she just disappeared. And I think that's when I started to hate that word, love. Now this… I need to work."

Mason looked up at his client. This was one of a few times he was happy to be an attorney, to defend someone worthwhile being pushed under by an unjust and spiteful adversary.

"I am going to tell you this…," Mason said. "She probably did love you – intensely. But she also loves survival. It's just how they are. She chose survival."

"Eventually they all choose survival," Squire sighed. "They just don't see it in me."

* * *

HE THREW his keys down on the counter and crawled onto the couch. With only a pillow to comfort him, he cried like he never had. What was it about him that women couldn't want? Why was it so easy to get a girlfriend and so hard to keep one? He wondered what other men had. They worked like crazy to get with women. They did stunts and performed like idiots. They chased money and careers to the point of being so singular-minded that Squire could barely listen to them as they sat at the bar lamenting about their lives. But they all had wives at home. They all told him how happy they were between sips of booze and distant stares. They looked miserable, all telling him that he should find someone like they had. It was the best thing they did. Happy wives and happy lives, however that cliché went.

The waitresses couldn't walk anywhere near them without their eyes locking on their asses and breasts. They made little comments about what they would do to them and laughed together. Squire watched and heard all of it and it sickened him. It just seemed like a bunch of sad men posturing some skill with women they never had. Every one of them had the same story about how they dated their wives and it always began and ended with their wallets.

He had tried it. He found women on apps and took them out on dates until he realized *app* really meant appetizers for her and a few drinks while she pigeoned-holed him into the group of basic, normal men who understood the long game better than he did. Then there were the others...

He remembered one in particular. His profile must have resonated somewhere very low in her abdomen because within ten minutes on a Sunday morning outside a coffee shop they were making out. He pushed the encounter as far as he felt a lucky man would have then sent her home, hoping he had done enough to see her again. It brought nothing.

The realization that she wanted him right then or never still sat in his mind adding fuel to a burning sense of inadequacy. She wanted a fuck toy for the day. That's all he felt like to her and so many others and that was all he was beginning to suspect he would ever be.

CHAPTER 10

Victoria ran the file across her nails like she was trying to erase them. Where was Howard? Date night had been his idea even before the revelation of Squire McDermott; now it was mandatory. Her perfume permeated the living room as she sat waiting, filing. She heard the garage door opening, the rumble of his Porsche. Like a good, obedient soldier she rose to meet him. Howard slipped in through the kitchen keeping the counter between them, he blurted out something about a quick shower as he dodged his way to the master bath. Through the fog of her bouquet she took in the faint hint of another.

"We are going to the club tonight," he announced as steam flowed through the crack in the door. She heard the hair dryer go to full blow. He would be out in minutes and ready to leave. For a moment, she hoped the hot air would dislodge the plugs he so loved. The dryer routine was new. His beards extended and retracted with the seasons while the little flaps over his chest drooped to peek down at the regal expanse of a stomach he never seemed to notice for what it was – a prize for a life well-managed, something to show for his success. She resigned herself to it and everything else that came with her life: the Mercedes, the jewelry, the house, the country club, the house cleaners, all of it. Everything beneath that was invisible or at worse a momentary nuisance to her reality.

Victoria looked at herself in the mirror. The dress ran over her ass perfectly, her breasts stood on point, showing the way forward with just enough cleavage showing. She inspected little wrinkles forming around her eyes hopelessly trying to reveal her age. Howard rarely mentioned anything, but when she complained his comment was always the same, "If you want to fix that..." She did. She wanted everything fixed.

* * *

MEAGAN TOOK Stephen's hand as he helped her from the Corvette. It took a feat of strength in her thighs to rise up out of it. As she stood, it seemed absurd to tower over something so powerful and fast. She thought about Victoria's testimony as the maître d' led them to their table. She felt self-conscious, as if all eyes were on her, judging her. It was an illusion, no one knew nor cared as much as she thought they should. She spent most of the day thinking about the days to come. So far the local press focused on Squire, portraying him as morally depraved and manipulative. Meagan knew in her heart they had it wrong. Under his charm and his looks, he had a beautiful soul. He was effortless, unassuming, living every moment distinctly. Maybe that was what scared her about him.

Meagan wondered why she couldn't forget him and just move on. There was something otherworldly about him, his touch, and how he had made her feel – safe and enthralled and reckless all at once. There was a frequency of his being that resonated, harmonized within her. She could hardly bear the days in court knowing what he must think of her. But soon it would be over. She could try to forget Squire ever happened and have time to focus on herself and her family. It would be time to feel grateful for Stephen.

* * *

THE COVER BAND was elegantly dressed playing the oldies. Members swayed and tapped their feet as Howard led her out to the car. He had the look in his eye. His hand rested on her thigh between the shifts as the Porsche sped through the dark towards home. The gate dutifully flowed out of their way as Howard let out the clutch. His anticipation expressed itself as the car lurched forward towards the garage.

Victoria went straight for her changing room to take off her earrings; she felt him behind her. His hands cupped her breasts. He kissed her neck. She felt his teeth clasp on the zipper as red chiffon fell from her shoulders. Victoria spun towards her husband. She could tell what he wanted, revenge through her dutiful submission. It was what she would give him.

With a grunt he penetrated her. His arms pushed her legs apart pinning her in a contorted split below his frantic thrusting. Victoria's mind wandered off, her eyes shut tight. He was relentless. The bulk of his stomach thumped her before the slap of his thrusts echoed in the room. It was taking him longer than usual. Maybe it was the drinks she could still smell on him. In the rare moment when they would have sex twice in a day, his second go at it would always take longer. All these things ran through her head as he kept going then he paused and stared down into her eyes, "Did you cum?" he asked.

Victoria thought quickly, "Not yet but I am close" He resumed.

She knew how to release him. The wails and moans rose out of her chest like the rehearsed sermon of an evangelist. She would stir him into biblical ecstasy. He met her tones with his own. In the moment she looked for, her nails bit deep into the skin on his ass as she shrieked. His pumping slowed and came to a stop. He had conquered any doubt. She was still his.

* * *

SQUIRE LAY in bed thinking about whether he should get a new cat, or maybe a dog. *Lifestyle*, he thought, *cats are easier.* It felt good to be alone. *Maybe I should wait.* An anxious thought rushed at him all of a sudden. What was going to happen if he lost? How would he pay the settlement? There must be ways, maybe in increments. For a moment he thought about texting Elizabeth. He hadn't heard from her in a while. They sort of stopped calling each other almost as quickly as they had gotten together. It was the day she asked if he had any other positions he liked and if he had any kinks. He really didn't. It seemed like too much to connect with someone deeply and focus on fulfilling a goal of sexual adventurism.

Besides his mild spinner fetish, his only real kink was an idea of love he now thought no woman was capable of understanding through explanation or her intuition. Explaining it would never work. It seemed like the most off-putting thing he could ever do. It had to be demonstrated. Maybe that was the problem with kinks, they all seemed like they needed to be explained, directed, and negotiated – their script followed. Was that it? Was that the problem?

He had never had to negotiate sex, never recalled actually asking for it. It just happened enough to become somewhat expected if not from *her* then from *her* or *her*. It was part of his life, it came unconsciously like breathing. And now, he was alone on a Friday night wondering what color cat he should get. It wasn't even worth going out. Friday was date night. All the women had their itineraries lined up. Saturday was better for meeting women. He knew it never mattered for him; every day and every night brought them on the wind. He felt exhausted, tired of everything.

Everything OK?

At least his attorney give a shit about him. *Yeah, I'm OK*, he replied. *What're you up to?*

Sitting at the bar, come out

Squire thought better of it but something prodded him out of bed. *On the way*

"What do you want? I'm buying," Mason asked as Squire sat.

"Glenfiddich, double."

* * *

MEAGAN LEANED ON HER ELBOWS. At least he could sort of hit that spot if she arched her back just right. And there was something freeing about not having to look at Stephen, at least not yet. She felt ashamed of herself for what she was doing. She felt him pull out then came the a pressure she didn't want. "No!" she exclaimed as she looked back over her shoulder. "Not tonight. It hurts."

"Did it hurt when he did it?"

She kicked at him and screamed until he fell back off the bed. "Fuck you!" she yelled.

"The kids, Meagan," Stephen tried to calm her.

"Fuck you," she growled angrily, her clenched hand came up under his chin ready to strike. With a push she got past him and locked herself in the bathroom. She could hear him scuffle out into the dark, quiet house making the rounds, checking if the children had heard.

She sat naked on the toilet, cold and crying. There was a timid knock and a whimper of her name. She turned on the shower, slipped into the therapy of the hot, pelting stream. Her head against the tile, she cried.

"Meagan?" she could hear through the door until he gave up.

He was feigning sleep, facing away. She slipped into her side of the bed, avoiding the touch and feel of any part of him. Stephen turned to her; his face looked repentant, submissive.

"I'm sorry," he said. "I didn't mean to say that."

She breathed in, held it. His hand sheepishly came to rest on her stomach. She didn't resist. She knew he needed to touch her to make himself feel contrite.

"He never did that. You should know that. He never wanted to and I hate it."

"You never told me you hated it," Stephen replied quietly.

"I thought it was something I had to do for you."

"What made you think that?" Stephen said as he propped his head up higher on the pillow.

"I don't know. I don't want to talk about it. I don't want to talk about him," she grumbled.

"OK," Stephen whispered. With a last regretful look into her eyes, he rolled away.

CHAPTER 11

"Call your next witness, Mr. Devine."

"Thank you, Judge, I would like to call Mr. John G. Davis to the stand," Woodrow P. Devine announced. Mason leaned back in his chair and watched as the Evangelical Family Counselor marched to the stand. The man's eyes closed briefly taking in the spirit as his hand came to rest on the Bible.

"Mr. Davis," Woodrow began, "please tell us about your expertise as well as your relationship with the plaintiffs."

"Where do I begin? I have a Masters Degree in Christian Counseling from the Rosemont Union Evangelical Seminary. Over twenty years I have counseled hundreds of couples within our congregation. However, I am open to anyone who seeks the guidance of our Lord and Savior Jesus Christ within their holy, matrimonial union. I think I have seen it all: the transgressions, the lies, the evil temptations that befall us. As for my clients, the Rogerses, they came to me seeking to understand how this could happen to a union fortified in Christ. We had conjoint sessions as well as one-on-ones. The Rogerses have given me permission to discuss their matter openly before the court. Our Lord knows all and all shall be forgiven." He handed a letter to the bailiff.

"Amen," Mason whispered. "Lord have mercy upon his wretched soul."

"Mr. Davis, tell the court what, in your expertise, brings a Christian family to this sinful state?"

"Objection, Your Honor," Mason said calmly. "The phrase, *sinful state*, is a value judgement. It's prejudicial and biased."

"Judge, with all *due* respect to the defense, a family who begins with and lives within their faith is surrounded and tempted by sin outside of that faith. The state of departure from the sanctity of their union is a sinful state."

"Mr. Devine," Judge Perkins replied, "this is a court of law not a religious inquisition. Proceed from that framework... Sustained."

"Judge, if I may approach?" Woodrow P. Devine asked. Mason groaned as he pushed himself up out of a slouch he had finally found comfortable.

"Mr. Devine," Judge Perkins said, "what is your point? And make it quick."

"Judge," Woodrow whispered, "moral framework is the foundation of a healthy marriage. I think everyone knows that. Moral framework comes from inside oneself, from one's heart and from one's spirit, as well as service to a higher being and cause, not solely from the fear of man-made legal repercussions.

"Although the Family Unity Sustainment Act has grey area morality within it, it means to protect families from the outside influence that would harm the union, which in turn is the collective morality within that union. Therefore, it is, in my opinion, naturally biased in favor of a moral standard to protect our country from the depravity of sinfulness and the sinful state we are all tempted to enter into from time to time. We have many examples of law in the United States that blend morality and legal control."

"Such as?" the Judge asked, "I know what they are but give me an example."

"Blue laws, drug laws, laws imposed on various goods and services deemed to be harmful yet enticing to our citizens," Devine paused, "prostitution."

"You made your point," Judge Perkins scowled. "Mr. Braddock?"

"I'm sold, Your Honor," Mason grinned. He caught a squinted, suspicious look leering down at him before he and Woodrow were waved away.

"Mr. Devine," Judge Perkins announced, "you may proceed. Please keep your questioning within relevance to this trial and not on some moral crusade." Mason laughed out loud. The judge slammed his gavel down and pointed it at him. "And I remind you, Mr. Braddock, you have a duty to defend your client. You are not here for your amusement." The gavel smashed down again, the sound block flew off the bench while Mason bit into his lips trying to control himself. Even Squire began to loosen up for the first time. Mr. John G. Davis sat rigid, hands on his lap, expressionless like a lump of Christmas coal.

"Is that guy alive?" Mason leaned over to whisper to Squire.

"He's all puffed up with the Holy Spirit," Squire replied. Mason lost it. The judge glared at him, called a short break and threw his gavel on the bench.

As Judge Perkins emerged from his chambers, they rose, they sat, the court session re-began. John G. Davis looked like he hadn't moved. "God, that guy creeps me out," Mason whispered.

"Mr. Davis, again I thank you for sharing your time with us today," Woodrow P. Devine opened.

Davis hinged his rigid frame forward towards the microphone, "It is the Lord's time I give."

"Jesus F'ing Christ," Mason whispered. Judge Perkins cleared his throat, glanced at Devine and Davis then stared directly at Mason. He would not take another break, someone was going to be held in contempt.

"Mr. Davis, in your own words, please describe what happened to bring the Rogerses to you."

Again the pelvis pivoted the rigid upper torso towards the microphone, "They came to me due to Mrs. Rogers' transgression. Their hope, they shared with me, was to find peace and forgiveness and continue their marriage in the arms of a forgiving Father, Son, and Holy Ghost."

Mason lassoed and tamed an *Amen* before it could escape his lips. Davis took a deep breath, "Her transgression was similar to that of Eve. In place of knowledge, the forbidden fruit of lust was brandished before her by a tempting demonic force in the shape and shell of a man. Satan is but a handsome angel befallen and cursed by our Lord. Be it he, who was but a demon, who enticed the lustful thirst of Mrs. Rogers in a moment of her weakness in herself, in her marriage, and in our Lord and Savior Jesus Christ. Only Lucifer is such as he who descends upon the righteous and innocent when the armor of their faith has been drawn thin." Judge Perkins looked directly at Mason, gavel ready.

"What was the therapy you gave to the Rogerses?" Devine asked.

"We focused on scripture."

"Specifically? Is there a passage that you recall that had healing effects?"

"*Therefore do not let sin reign in your mortal body, that you should obey it in its lusts. And do not present your members as instruments of unrighteousness to sin, but present yourselves to God as being alive from the dead, and your members as instruments of righteousness to God. For sin shall not have dominion over you, for you are not under law but under grace...* Romans 6: 12-14," he blurted out.

Davis leaned back, took another deep breath, and resumed before Woodrow P. Devine could get to his next question, *"Flee from sexual immorality. All other sins a man commits are outside his body, but he who sins sexually sins against his own body. Do you not know that your body is a temple of the Holy Spirit, who is in you, whom you have received from God? You are not your own; you were bought at a price. Therefore honor God with your body.* 1st Corinthians 6: 18-20"

"You were bought at a price..." Devine repeated. "Can you elaborate on that?"

"Certainly, it is the price that our Lord and Savior Jesus Christ paid for our transgressions," Davis answered.

The gavel fell, "Mr. Devine, this is not a church..."

"Judge, respectfully," Woodrow P. Devine spoke up, "we are establishing that their marital union and the vows they took within their church in front of God and witnesses are just as binding now as when they took them. Their belief that Jesus died for and paid for their sins is tantamount to their faith and thus their marriage.

"Not only are their lives bought at a price but their marriage and everything they are and have is bought at a price. That price was paid for on the cross and whoever shall stand between the sacrifice of our Lord, our Redeemer, the rightful, righteous owner of our souls, commits the foulest of transgressions against not only themselves but our Savior as well."

"Do you have any idea how close I am to throwing this case out, Mr. Devine?" Judge Perkins glared down at him. "Mr. Braddock?"

"Your Honor," Mason spoke up, "I am not opposed to the moral, religious nature of the questioning the plaintiffs are using to convince this court. But I yield completely to your discretion."

"Then proceed, Mr. Devine," Judge Perkins muttered.

"Mr. Davis, we have established the religious framework for your work with the Rogerses, can you tell us, in your expertise, what makes a happy spouse commit adultery?"

"I think there are many factors but they all are rooted in the same distancing from a morally driven life in Christ. In the case of the Rogerses, it was momentary weakness that unfortunately met in meeting the defendant. I think it is already known that the defendant is a bartender and he met Mrs. Rogers at the bar where he served her. This is a normal locale of a predator." Woodrow turned towards the defense, expecting an attack. Mason sat still; his head spun with rhetoric waiting for a better time.

"We will all directly face Satan at some point in our lives…" Davis said as he leered at the defense.

"Mr. Davis, you met with the Rogerses one-on-one as well as together. How were they together?"

"There was love, there was togetherness. It was obvious that they love each other. And if I might add, in her one-on-one sessions, Mrs. Rogers expressed her love for Stephen most emphatically. She was contrite as much as or beyond anyone else I have counseled. She asked for forgiveness and offered to be baptized. She wishes to publicly express and renew her faith in our Lord and his gift of salvation just as Stephen has."

"She had not been baptized before?" Devine asked.

"She has, but it is not uncommon to be baptized again when someone recommits themselves to our Lord and Savior Jesus Christ. Her original baptism as a child served to wash away inherited original sin. She could not know its real significance then..."

"So, do you think that this experience has brought the Rogerses closer to each other and to Christ?"

"Not without some underlying damage that they will work through for many, many years. It is this that brings the transgression to this courtroom. It saddens me that we are here but evil must be confronted."

"Thank you, Mr. Davis. No further questions, Your Honor," Woodrow P. Devine said as he straightened his notes giving them a punctuating smack upon the lectern.

"Mr. Davis," Mason said as he walked towards the witness, "Is this a Christian country?"

"I believe it to be."

"According to the Constitution, it is not," Mason replied. "Other than the Signing Clause where the scribe, Jacob Shallus, inserted *in the year of our lord* there is no mention of a deity and certainly nothing specifically about Christianity."

"I don't think that matters. The Founding Fathers expressed their religions quite openly in their lives and in the Declaration Of Independence," Davis rebutted. "The Constitution served to unify the States. Most of the States had adopted a specific order of denomination of Christianity that reflected the majority of their citizens. The Constitution would not declare one denomination or another out of respect for the individual powers of the States. Other than Rhode Island, they all wrote our Lord and Savior into their Constitutions in one way or another."

"That is true, Mr. Davis, but in our modern form, our government does not have an official religion, correct?"

"Legally correct but you cannot deny that God has no part: In God we trust, the Pledge Of Allegiance, prayers before political sessions, et cetera," Davis shot back. "Ignoring God, does not make God disappear from our lives, our hearts, our existences... You can make the case that our government is second only to God in whom it derives its authority."

"Let me ask you this," Mason continued, "do you believe that someone has to have a belief in God in order to live a moral, ethical life?"

"Yes, I do," Davis replied.

"You believe that it is imperative that someone has a belief in God and therefore, after that, one has the potential to lead a moral and ethical life, is that what you are saying? And secondarily, the belief precedes the morality, correct?"

"That is correct," Davis squirmed, "I believe they go hand in hand regardless of which one precedes the other."

"With all due respect, Mr. Davis, that is not what you said. One must precede the other in your opinion."

"It is the commandment of our God, our Lord and Savior that we act morally and the actions we take are moral because we are commanded to be so," Davis said.

"Is an action good because God commands it or is it a command of God that it is good?"

"God is goodness and perfect, we are not," Davis replied.

"I appreciate your skill at avoiding the question," Mason retorted.

"Objection!" Woodrow yelled. "He's badgering the witness."

"Sustained. Mr. Braddock, try to refrain from your badgering if you can."

"Mr. Davis, do you believe in freewill?"

"Of course I do, we are fallen, imperfect. We make mistakes and it is only through Jesus that we are saved."

Mason hesitated, a thought seemed to come to him, "What about evolution and natural reproductive impulses within us?"

"Reproduction is commanded by God, sanctified by him

within the framework of marital union. *Marriage should be honored by all, and the marriage bed kept pure, for God will judge the adulterer and all the sexually immoral.* Hebrews 13:4"

Mason replied, *"You have heard that it was said, 'You shall not commit adultery.' But I tell you that anyone who looks at a woman lustfully has already committed adultery with her in his heart.* Matthew 5: 27-28."

He looked directly at Davis, "Can you explain why the women always seem to be the victims and never the instigators in adultery within scripture especially when they go to great lengths to sexualize themselves and extract lustful attention?"

"That is not true," Davis interrupted. Mason's smile grew cold, waiting. If he knew anything about evangelicals, it was their innate ability to evangelize themselves into a trap.

"Please explain," Mason replied.

"Adultery in the Bible is a crime committed, as discussed in the Old Testament, against another man. An adulterous woman commits the crime against her husband."

"Thank you Mr. Davis, could you tell the court why it is a crime affecting men?"

Davis hesitated then blurted out, "Because a man's lineage, honor, and possessions are affected."

"One of his possessions is his wife in this scenario, is she not?"

"She is." Davis sulked.

"So, what you are saying is that the woman's crime is against her husband, the man involved with her commits adultery against her husband, and the husband is the ultimate victim because his possession has been damaged," Mason grinned.

"Yes, that is what the Bible says."

"Who is the victim when the biblical, Old Testament man commits adultery with someone such as a prostitute?"

"According to scripture, there is no victim," Davis replied. His rigid frame began to slump.

"According to scripture," Mason interrupted, *"If a man is found lying with the wife of another man, both of them shall die, the man who lay with the woman, and the woman. So you shall purge the evil from Israel.* Deuteronomy 22:22. There is no provision for the woman, no recourse if, say, a married man were lay with another upon the bed as long she is unmarried. The scripture ignores women. They cannot protest the infidelity of their husbands. Wives are the possessions of men." Mason looked at Davis, waiting.

"That's essentially correct," Davis muttered, "in scripture."

"What does the Bible say about kinks, sexual exploration and the like?"

"1st Corinthians 6:18; *Flee from sexual immorality. All other sins a person commits are outside the body, but whoever sins sexually, sins against their own body,*" Davis sputtered.

Mason looked down at his notes, *"Do you not know that your bodies are members of Christ himself? Shall I then take the members of Christ and unite them with a prostitute? Never! Do you not know that he who unites himself with a prostitute is one with her in body? For it is said, 'The two will become one flesh.' But whoever is united with the Lord is one with him in spirit.*

"Then as you said and I will elaborate, *Flee from sexual immorality. All other sins a person commits are outside the body, but whoever sins sexually, sins against their own body.*

"That is where you stopped. It goes on: *do you not know that your bodies are temples of the Holy Spirit, who is in you, whom you have received from God? You are not your own; you were bought at a price. Therefore honor God with your bodies.* 1st Corinthians 15-20."

"Would you say that this is what the Bible offers as a definition of sexual conduct outside of baby-making? I assume the phrase, *members of Christ,* is referring to all of the *members* including the phallic synonym for *member*. You know, penis. Oh, and fingers...And heads, shoulders, knees, and toes. Knees and toes...or whatever you might be into." The gallery laughed as Davis shivered over the thought of an unsavory interpretation. Judge Perkins snarled.

"Did Mr. or Mrs. Rogers discuss their kinks with you? A penchant for buggery or something of the like?" Mason looked over at Woodrow waiting for an objection, nothing. *"The men of Sodom were wicked and sinners exceedingly before the Lord.* Genesis 13:13," Mason recited.

"Or maybe this one, *Just as Sodom and Gomorrah and the surrounding cities, which likewise acted immorally and indulged in unnatural lust, serve as an example by undergoing a punishment of eternal fire.* Jude 7"

* * *

SHE LEVITATED her hips under him, her finger nails dug into his ass pulling him into her harder and harder. He slipped out, she pulled then winced, "Not that, not yet," Meagan gasped.

He knew what she meant as he glided back deep inside her. He knew she liked it when he slowly went from out to fully in but she looked distracted; something was wrong and he knew what it was. He slowed his pace, gently continuing to pump and brought his body down flat upon hers. Only his elbows bore his weight to keep from crushing her. Her hips responded, circling along with his, "It's OK, I'm not really into that," Squire whispered. "Hand me that pillow."

With one hand he lifted her up off the bed, slipping the pillow under her ass, her ankles rest on his shoulders as he move rhythmically inside her. "Oh my god," she moaned. "Yes..." For the way he was built, this position always worked. The g-spot was real and he knew exactly where it was. In some women, it seem to run around hiding. On Meagan, it was obvious. You just had to trust in it and she had to trust in you. It didn't take her long to cum, the consistency of his rhythm against that precious little spot.

He fell off to her side as she breathed in and out deeper than he had ever seen her. Her heart raced. His hands clasped behind his head; he waited. With a pounce she came to, rolling onto him, kissing his neck, his chest, fondling him. "I want you to cum," she whispered in his ears. "I want to watch you cum on my breasts."

He started slowly, his hand ran up and down. Meagan watched intently, reaching over the take him in her hand, in her mouth. She knew when he would get there. She would help him. She put his hand back; the stroking gained pace. She laid back just in time to catch the stream she asked for across her chest. Her fingers ran through it, circling its warmth around her nipples as he lay back down on the pillow.

"Squire, I love you," she whispered. "Thank you for understanding."

"Understanding?" he asked.

"The butt, I hate it."

"It's OK, so do I," he replied. She took him, pulled him to her and held him. He could feel the thumping of her heart against his pecs. He pushed back, kissed her deeply and slipped away to the shower. She followed.

* * *

"ANAL, MR. DAVIS," Mason said as he tried to remain as clinical as possible. "Do the Rogerses enjoy anal stimuli together? And who pokes who, or is it whom? I can never get that right."

Before Woodrow could object Davis reacted, "I wouldn't know. Perhaps the Rogerses mentioned it."

"So you *do* know," Mason shot back.

"There are some things that should remain private, even in this forum."

"Thank you, Mr. Davis," Mason smirked. "No further questions." He gave a long look towards the jury as he sat. The women all looked slightly uncomfortable, the men incredulous.

CHAPTER 12

"Your Honor, the defense calls its first witness," Mason turned to watch as she stepped through the gate and into the well. Her eyelashes batted as she looked at Squire. The rest of her was tense. Her reluctance to testify was ground down into a fine powder and blown away over weeks of subtle and not so subtle hounding. Mason had taken her to dinner, to more expensive dinners then to the mall to shop. His efforts were blatant and unethical. But here she was – little, spunky, and still so seductive.

"Miss Hakobyan, please approach the witness stand and be sworn in," Judge Perkins smiled. She was difficult to ignore. There was something about her, those seductive eyes, that tiny, firm body and the way she walked. Her skirt flowed without a breeze, always in motion. The way it ran down, hovering over her ass, hiding the obvious tempting thought of what those legs must look like. A man with large hands could nearly join his fingers around her waist. And everything about her was proportioned... What the Turks had done to try and exterminate then expel a bloodline that created Lilly Hakobyan, was sinister.

Squire sat quietly thinking back. She was different than the rest. He still had no understanding why he and Lilly weren't married, shuttling around little, beautiful copies of her. He watched her take her seat. She looked over at him again. He looked for a ring.

She wasn't married; no ring and she would have said another name. *What happened?* he thought. Was it worth it to watch her fade off into the future when there was nothing really wrong with them together at the time? Seven years and she still looked the same. Why hadn't he fought a little harder?

Mason stood, "Miss Hakobyan, could you state your full name please."

"Lilly Zabelle Hakobyan," the name rolled off her sweet little tongue. Squire looked at the jury. The men were sitting straighter; the women appeared apprehensive.

"For the court, please tell us how you met Squire McDermott."

"We met at a bar. I mean he met me at a bar. I was with a group of people I know. We were all in a group and he was there and I was there and we were all talking but we didn't talk that much but, you know, we did talk and he was in one of my college classes and I could tell that he liked me. He is really cute, you know, but I wasn't really into having a boyfriend or anything at the time, or maybe I did have one. I don't remember but it seemed like he liked me and wanted more than I wanted but, you know, we just met so there wasn't going to be anything, at least not then but we kept talking when I wasn't talking to someone else. It was kind of a weird time for me. My dad had just died but that wasn't really what the problem was because my parents were divorced and my mom really sort of hated my dad and me and my sister were living with her and she made us not like him too but he died…"

"You met him at a bar?" Mason interrupted.

Oh God, that was it, Squire thought. It all came back. That was it, the periodic, incessant rambling. She was the verbal excuse for flood control but she was so sweet and kind and the horniest women he had ever known. Sometimes the words would not stop unless extreme action was taken. Other times she said very little, especially when she was up to something.

* * *

"Squire," she whispered in his ear. "Look at that…"

A little breeze blew the tops of overgrown grass where the horses hadn't grazed for a month. Above, the Perseids streaked across the sky, Northern Lights danced above the Arctic along the dark, treed horizon.

He hadn't seen or spoken to her in ten months. Out of the blue, she called and somewhere between a deluge of words there had been a reflective calm, "Can you take me out to your parents farm to see the meteors?"

Reluctantly, he agreed. She was a friend, nothing had ever happened between them. They had gone out together for a while – at least four or five times a month. It was mostly on Friday nights but they weren't together.

Since their first meeting she had acquired a new boyfriend although Squire had never met him. They had no common friends, just each other. The only proof of boyfriend Squire had seen was a picture, a completely normal guy bordering on chubby, the kind of man who can never seem to burn off his baby fat. He worked for a chain of restaurants as an area operations manager or something like that, something normal and respectable. That's all Squire knew; he had no interest in investigating. The only thing he had ever wondered was if she talked to the boyfriend the way she talked to him. God help the guy if she did.

Through her, Squire had come to realize the power a woman had in a club. If he was a natural with women anywhere else, in those settings he was almost useless. There was too much white noise of sound and attention, too many drunk men sidling up on the women to buy them drinks and flex their willingness to capitulate. When he was with her, it was as if men could sense that he and Lilly weren't official or really much of anything but friends and they took action.

"Wow," she whispered. "I'm a little cold." Her little body pressed harder against him as he adjusted the blanket. She sat between his legs innocently representing their history. Squire held her like a boyfriend feeling like a brother. The dichotomy of the feelings gave him the creeps but by now they were so platonic, so familiar with each other, her position nor her touch stirred an ounce of arousal within him. They simply sat, watching the streaks of light, the dancing crimson and violet to the north. There was hardly any conversation, no longing gazes at each other, not a heavy sigh, nothing, just together and comfortable…

He could feel how relaxed she was, her back melting into his chest; her head tipped back upon his shoulder. The tickle of her hair on his neck seemed more of a nuisance than a nudge.

The last time they were out together he caught her giving him a jealous, scolding evil eye as he stepped away from the boys jockeying to entertain her. A cute blond, stepped up, "Is that your girlfriend? Why aren't you defending her?"

Squire laughed, "She can handle it. God help them if they try to handle her."

"You're not jealous?"

"Not really," he replied. He could feel the challenge, the

evaluation. "She's kinda cute, isn't she?" he said as he winked at Lilly.

"Yeah, she's alright," the girl replied looking Lilly up and down. "I don't think she likes you talking to me."

"I like to piss her off once in a while," Squire grinned. "It's worth it. Makes me feel alive."

Lilly gave him a look he had rarely seen, anger. Her eyes shifted back and forth from the blond to Squire. As one of the men stepped in blocking her view, he took his new friend by the hand and led her to the other side of the bar out of Lilly's sight. On the way home she sulked. "Who was that?" she asked. "Did you know her?"

"I will tomorrow," he grinned.

"I hate you," she sighed. Squire laughed.

"Wow, did you see that one?" Squire's voice hummed quietly in her ear. She took in a deep breath and pulled his arm around her. *She feels safe with me*, Squire thought. *She should, I haven't tried to get with her in forever.*

It came suddenly. She spun towards him, pinned him down and stared directly into his eyes before her lips fell on his. He tensed, he was reluctant, the lust for her he had embedded under years of platonic denial finally gave way. He gripped her tiny ass in his hands as they kissed frantically trying to swallow each other. It was hurried and violent the way they struggled, making up for years of pent up longing.

She reached down, yanked his pants off and took him in her mouth. Her hand cupped him as her tongue ran up and down. He was stunned. He felt an inclination to pull back, ease up. There was something in him thinking they should slow down but the dam between them had broken and she was a raging flood. Her shirt flew off into the front seat. She straddled him writhing up and down as he tried to suck in a whole breast, his tongue and teeth grabbing at her nipples.

"Oh god," he sighed intently as his hands brought her up

and down helping her ride him. Up and down, over and over, their bodies wet with the sweat of a steamy August night and fervent lovemaking.

How quickly it had gone from détente to all out aggression. He threw her down on the backseat, the thong he had pushed to the side was ripped off her and thrown out the window. As he pummeled her hard, her hands leveraged against the car door forcing herself toward him to meet his thrusts. There was nothing sweet about them. They were raw, aggressively trying to kill each other with every push until they both came together gasping with exhaustion. Squire leaned back opposite her, their heads each claiming a side of the backseat.

She reached for him taking what he had left in her hand. He felt her rubbing herself with him, pushing him in pulling him out like he was her toy. She was vivacious, satiated but still feeling hungry. He tried to sit up to retake her. She pushed him back down into the scissor position she demanded. He hadn't thought he was capable of the angle, maybe it was a circumstance of his semi-softening. Normally he stood straight up towards the sky but somehow she had him wrenched over under her control as she used him.

All he could do was watch her little fingers, wrapped around him. Her chest heaved up and down as she slapped him against her, wiggled him against her clitoris, stuck him in, yanked him out, and slapped herself again. If there had been neighbors within earshot to hear her, they would have grabbed their guns and come running. It was the most feral sex Squire had ever experienced and for a while it would become their normal.

"Miss Hakobyan," Squire snapped back to the present as Mason questioned her. "You said, 'he just gets it.' What did you mean by that? What is *it*?"

"Um," she thought, "I don't know how to explain it."

"Do you think there is something about Squire's ability to relate to women?"

"Objection! Your Honor, he can't lead his witness like that," Devine complained.

"The jury will disregard the question. Sustained. Rephrase your question without leading her. You may proceed, Mr. Braddock."

"Miss Hakobyan, to the best of your ability, try to describe what you mean by, 'he just gets it,'"

"Well," she hesitated, Squire squirmed, "there is something he does and I don't think he knows what it is. But you know, it's something maybe from his childhood or something like that where he, you know, maybe tries to relate to women on our level but even as a man he doesn't do it like he is trying. It's like he just gets it and, whatever that is, is something we get and it's really hard to explain but you know we all get it. I am speaking for all women, I guess. I think we all sort of get it deep down." She looked up, the whole courtroom was watching intently. The few journalists left in the gallery stopped scribbling and stared at her.

As Mason was about to speak she resumed, "And you know he doesn't try. Did I say that? I mean, it's like he doesn't have to try. And he is cute, he is so cute. He is really cute like all the time but he doesn't try to be cute." Lilly paused to take in a breath, "But you know sometimes that doesn't really work because being cute is one thing and just getting it is another. It's sort of like he knows how to be cute and be a man, like a real man and sometimes he's a total asshole but it's natural and even that sometimes is cute and it's mostly kind of hot all the time. Ask anyone how hot that is. They will tell you. Anyone who has ever been with him will tell you. It's so hot sometimes. That's what *it* was when we were together even though we weren't together very long I sort of got that he got *it* but then something happened and then I was confused even though I don't think he changed. Maybe it was me. I don't know. Anyway, like I was saying, he just get's it. I think all the women know he gets it. It sort of comes out of him without trying. He doesn't try. He doesn't have to but if you were a woman you would understand like I said before…"

Mason tapped the lectern, held up his hand for Lilly to stop, "Focusing on *it*, what is this thing called *it*?"

"Oh, that's easy to explain," Lilly's cute little head tipped, her eyelashes fluttered. "*It* is it. It just is. And Squire gets that but he doesn't know he gets that." Her arms crossed, she leaned back and gave Squire the look he knew so well. *It* needed no further explanation.

* * *

"OH MY GOD," she moaned, "you still have it. Oh god, oh god, fuck me harder Squire. You will never lose it." Lilly spun him onto his back, she mounted him reverse and pounded her ass against his stomach. There was nothing for him to do but watch the scene. That tiny round ass, revealing daylight towards his feet then slamming the door shut as she clamped down on him grinding a little twisting circle before rising to smash down again.

Just as he remembered something from her ramblings about gymnastics and the floor exercise, her ass flew into the air as she rose into a handstand split, hovering momentarily above his face. Then in a controlled descent, her clitoris stuck the landing on his lower lip as his apparatus landed between hers. His arms came up, locking her in place. They were enraptured as tongues and humming frantically batted at each other between quivering legs.

She left a note: *I really adore you, good luck with your trial. And thanks for letting me drive you home. Love, Lilly. Kisses*

* * *

Woodrow P. Devine had tried his best to cross-examine. He and all the other men in the room were trying to get to the bottom of *it*; the secret *it* of Squire McDermott. Only Lilly knew, and Meagan, and Victoria, and Monica and Brianna and…

But Devine gave it one last shot to force Squire into submission, "Miss Hakobyan, why did you and Squire McDermott stop seeing each other? Why no progress in the relationship?"

"Hmm, I don't know," she thought. "Maybe we had progressed as far as we could. I really don't know."

"So, whatever this *it* is. It doesn't seem to last very long." Woodrow grinned.

"That's not true. *It* haunts you. You may not be with him anymore but he is still somewhere deep inside you," Lilly exhaled. Her hand reached between her legs, taken over by the memory of Squire's *it*.

"No further questions, Your Honor," Woodrow P. Devine frowned.

CHAPTER 13

"Lilly drove you home?"

"Yeah," Squire smirked.

"You know that leaving your car in the lot here gets it towed," Mason replied.

"I do now."

"Jesus man, you don't have any money. What if we lose?" Mason shot back.

"We are not going to lose," Squire defended. "You're the one who is supposed to tell me that, right?"

Mason sighed. Squire was right, it was his job to keep the client positive even when things looked bleak. "You may call your witness, Mr. Braddock," Judge Perkins spoke up.

"Thank you, Your Honor," Mason said as he approached the lectern. "The defense calls Bryant Seward." As the former roommate was sworn in, Mason turned to Squire and whispered, "You're sure about this guy?"

Squire nodded, "Bro code. He's lightened up since he was my roommate. A lot…"

"Mr. Seward," Mason began, "please tell the court how

you know Mr. McDermott, how long you have known each other, and the nature of your relationship."

"Well, Squire and I were roommates for about three years. As far as the nature of our relationship, I would say we're still friends. We hang out sometimes."

"If you look around the room, do you recognize anyone?"

"Oh yeah, Meagan and Victoria for sure," Bryant grinned. He scanned the gallery looking for more familiar faces.

"So, you were present for their alleged affairs," Mason said. "What can you tell the court about that time?"

Bryant remembered a day Meagan came to the apartment. They met briefly before he slipped out to a club but the cookies she made for them in the weeks to come, they were the best. "They didn't really go out. They wanted to stay in and you know…"

"What?" Mason asked.

"Have sex," Bryant grinned. "That's all they did. I literally had to leave most of the time. It was just too loud. We had a cat at the time. The cat was freaked out. It used to sit there and look at me like I was supposed to do something to save it from the noise." Stephen Rogers looked at Meagan in disgust as she slunk down into her chair.

"What about the neighbors? Were they bothered?"

"Yes and no, we had pretty thick walls and by then he had sold the drum bed," Bryant laughed.

"The drum bed? Could you explain?"

Bryant's grin grew, "It was a bed he made with a huge drum built into the headboard. You know: boom, boom, boom. Some people like padding. It was sort of like that but boom, boom, boom… That thing drove the women and the neighbors tribal. Obviously for different reasons." The gallery laughed; Judge Perkins' hand went for the gavel.

"Would you say Squire and Meagan had a good relationship?"

"They did, she seemed to dig him and he really liked her. Then she told him she was married. They kept at it for a while but I think he knew it was going to be temporary. He isn't a cheating kind of guy, at least not with married women. I remember when they split. I don't think I ever saw him so down. He wasn't Squire."

"How did he take the knowledge that she was married?" Mason asked.

"I think he was in denial."

Woodrow P. Devine scribbled furiously into his notes. The testimony was going well for him so far. He always thought Mason was an idiot, half-assed attorney.

"Mr. Seward, did you ever have any conversations with either Meagan or Victoria regarding Squire?"

"I did with Victoria, a little with Meagan."

"Can you recall the nature of those conversations?"

"They both wanted to know if he was a player, you know a guy who gets with a lot of girls," Bryant replied.

"Why would they want to know that?"

"Objection!" Devine yelled. "Speculation."

"Sustained."

Mason thought how to reframe the question. "Do you think he is a player?" He waited, there was nothing from Devine.

"I think he gets laid a lot. I'm not sure how his dick can handle it," Bryant laughed. Squire cringed. The gallery erupted.

After smashing nearly everything within arms length flat, Judge Perkins leaned over the bench, "Mr. Seward, this is a court of law. Keep your answers professional and to the point. Mr. Braddock, you may proceed but I am warning you…"

Mason wondered what more he could do with Bryant. How much did he really know since Squire and the women had spent nearly all of their time in the bedroom? He remembered back in law school when his roommate was getting a Masters in Sociology and had too much time to date. All he seemed to do was drag girls back to the apartment. Without earplugs he heard everything, he saw almost nothing.

"Mr. Seward," Mason continued, "how would you characterize the relationship between Victoria Cullen and Squire McDermott."

"Wild and sexual," he replied. He couldn't help looking over at her. Her frown curved downward so distinctly she looked like a child had drawn a sad, angry clown face on her. Howard Cullen seethed. It wasn't the first time Bryant had seen that.

* * *

"Where the fuck is he?" Howard yelled through the door.

Bryant looked at the cat, the cat looked at the door as it thundered from the kicks. "Nobody is home right now," Bryant said in a squeaky voice. "Just me and my little Miss Kitty. Please go away now."

"Where the fuck is Squire McDermott?"

"Squire McWho?"

"Dermott, motherfucker! Open the door!"

"OK, but you can't hurt my kitty," Bryant squeaked. "Do you promise?"

"Promise what?"

"Do you promise?" Bryant watched through the peep hole as Howard Cullen backed away and ran towards the door, his body smashing against it. He backed away again, "Careful kitty, he's a-comin'." The door opened, Howard's momentum carried him through and into the wall where Bryant met him with a baseball bat. "Now I told you to not to hurt my kitty but look what you done. She's all frightened up. Now we have to go to kitty counseling. You just stay right there or I'll bash your skull in." He tapped the bat up under Howard Cullen's chin pulling him up to his knees.

Howard hands were raised. He faked submission then went for the bat but Bryant was quick. The blunt end rammed Howard in the solar plexus dropping him into a heaving mass on the floor. Bryant brought the bat above his head. Howard cowered.

"Now, Mister, you best be going now before me and kitty get to thinkin' up somethin' special for ya. If yur looking fer Squire, you done got the wrong the place. He don't shack up in these here parts no more. Maybe you can sue him. Did he take yer lady or somethin'? Dang it all, that boy. Dem girlies do like themselves some Squire. Now git!" The baseball bat swatted Howard Cullen's ass as he ran across the threshold.

"Hey dude, some dude came over looking for you."

"That was probably Victoria's husband, was he sort of stubby?" Squire asked.

"Yeah, stubby. That's him. Don't worry too much. I think I scared him. Told him to sue you," Bryant laughed into the phone.

"Sue me? For what?"

* * *

"How long would Victoria Cullen stay when she came over?" Mason asked.

"When she was there, she was there for hours. I could hear them giggle then things would go quiet then you know. The moaning and the screaming in Spanish. Papi, folla-me! Folla-me duro! Queras que te chupo? Folla-me, folla-me!" The gavel came down. Howard Cullen could barely contain his rage. The only thing keeping him seated was Victoria's firm grip on his crotch.

"Enough, Mr. Seward!" Judge Perkins complained. "The next graphic sexual outburst in any language, I will hold you in contempt."

"OK," Bryant whimpered. Howard Cullen glared at his wife. She dabbed at a little trickle of sweat running down her cleavage with her free hand and clenched the other until he shuddered.

"Can you describe what it is about Squire that makes women respond to him like this?"

"Oh, wow," Bryant looked woozy, "I don't know. That's some psychological stuff. I mean he's just Squire. They don't all fall down at his feet or anything but there are certain women who just can't leave him alone. It's like they have to have him. They have the need for his seed. I've seen it."

"Mr. Seward, would you call Squire McDermott a Pick Up Artist?"

"No," Bryant spit out.

"Objection! Leading!"

Mason laughed quietly. It was out there. He had effectively taken the question from Woodrow, objection or not. Judge Perkins instructed the jury to disregard.

"May I reframe this question, Your Honor?" Mason asked.

"Proceed, counsel."

"In your own words, Mr. Seward, please describe for the court any psychological techniques Mr. McDermott uses to entice women into a sexual relationship."

Bryant thought, "Man, I don't know. I have seen it work too many times. Trust me, I have wanted to find out what he does but I can't be him. He is Squire McDermott. Women, like I said, some women, a lot of women, just come after him. Mostly they cum over and over and over, repeatedly before…" The gavel raised, pointing at Bryant's head. Judge

Perkins looked like he wanted to kill someone. It smashed down.

"Five-minute recess, counsels in my chambers! Both of you, now!"

Squire doodled on his pad while Bryant stood up to stretch. He gave a long hard look at Howard Cullen, making a baseball bat gripping gesture followed by a mischievous grin. "Meow," he mouthed. Howard was trying his best to remain calm but when it came to his wife and his reputation, he was a lit fuse.

"Mr. Seward," Judge Perkins leaned over as he sat back behind the bench, "the next sexual innuendo, inappropriate comment, et cetera you make, you are going to jail. This is my courtroom not an internet porn chat."

"Bummer, dude," he replied. "That blows."

"Blow as it may, do you understand me?" Judge Perkins scowled. Bryant nodded nervously.

"I have no further questions for Mr. Seward, Your Honor."

"Mr. Devine, your witness."

Woodrow P. Devine stood eloquently as was his impression of himself. "Mr. Seward, do you know what a Pick Up Artist is?"

"I do," Bryant grinned.

"Explain it for the court, would you please?"

"Uhh, a PUA, those guys called pick up artists use game to get with women," he answered.

"And what is *game*, Mr. Seward?" Woodrow bellowed.

"Uh, man, I don't know how to explain it…"

"Try your best, Mr. Seward."

"I guess game is like tricks that work," Bryant replied.

"It is my understanding that *game* refers to manipulative tactics used to gain sexual encounters with women. And this is what Mr. McDermott was up to with my clients wasn't he,

Mr. Seward?" Devine's neck turned red, attempting to break the seal his collar had on it.

"No, no!" Bryant yelled. "He doesn't do anything!"

"Are you sure he is not so manipulative that you and my clients didn't notice? Is he that good? Is he that sinister?" Woodrow P. Devine was getting impatient.

"Order, order, order, order! That's it! We are done for the day! Mr. Seward, you may step down and never come back here! Mr. Devine!" the judge stared menacingly at Woodrow. Mason had to look away to try to contain his laughter. The only one who was unfazed by the exchange was Squire. He doodled on his pad through everything barely bothering to look up.

Mason leaned over, "Squire, you should try to look interested. The jury is watching you."

"Meh," he replied, "They're not watching me; they're watching you, remember? Besides, they've already made up their minds about me anyway. What difference does it make?"

* * *

SQUIRE WONDERED how Mason had found her; why she bothered to respond. He had given more of a description and circumstance than a name. It came up in casual conversation. Mason was convinced she had to testify.

It's the misfortune of anyone who overvalues romance to be a bartender in the Caribbean especially at a resort full of single, horny women. The plane came every week, unleashed its winter-pale human cargo then a week later came to scoop them up, now freshly tanned, hungover, and satiated. The whole process was on repeat.

She really needed this vacation. As she walked down the steps onto the airport ramp, her miniskirt blew up to reveal her thong to the warm ocean breeze and the eyes of the boys who had drunk everything the bar cart had to offer.

Squire sat with his friends waiting for guests to arrive. The resort was like a self-contained village: its own waterworks, its own power, everything to feed and entertain four hundred people for the week.

Every Friday, he and his friends waited. There were rules for fraternization and there were the rules of the general manager. Keep it discreet. Tactically the worst thing he could do was to hook up with someone right away. She would either dog him all week or dump him for another, or worse, disparage his name to the other guests, his boss, and the general manager.

He and his friends let things play out for a few days. Why not? They had all become tired and cynical of how easy sex was anyway. Women on vacation are the least picky they had ever experienced. The resort had been his training ground in his early twenties. Squire would like to blame his problems with keeping a woman on the resort but he knew that was a disingenuous scapegoat. Girls had always like him, it just took him longer than most boys to see it.

On the island, everything was laid out bare in front of him. It was one per week, sometimes two, rarely three. None of them had time to complain. They wanted to get as much out of him as he could give in a few days. As he and his friends put them back on the plane to New York or Los Angeles or Des Moines they would scribble their numbers, peck his cheek, and promise to keep in touch. "If you're ever in... Call me," they would say. It wasn't true. What happened on the island was for the sensation of vacation. New York, Los Angeles and Des Moines were for something completely different, a divergent female strategy.

He picked up her suitcase and heaved it up on his head, balancing it with one hand as he led her to her room. The speech was memorized, always the same: there's a meeting for new arrivals in the theater at 6:00. The restaurant is next to the theater which is next to the main pool. You can't miss it.

As he finished, as he was about to say, "if you need anything..." She spun towards him and yanked off her blouse, her miniskirt dropped to the floor, padding her knees. He felt his swim suit drop. She took him in her hand then her mouth. As he responded, the feeling of a condom sliding on made him wonder if he were dreaming.

In front of him she bent over the armchair in the corner waving her ass back and forth like a cat in heat, calling him in. He had no time to think, to calculate the absurdity of the seduction. As he entered her from behind, he thought: thirty-five seconds if you only count the welcome speech, maybe two minutes total with a quiet, mostly silent walk to her room.

What is going on here? he asked himself as his hips banged against her ass. She reached between her legs and grabbed him pulling him as he pushed. He loved that. How did she know? *Thirty-five seconds, she just got here, she's been off the plane not even an hour, thank god she's cute.* He couldn't imagine what kind of hell his week would be like if she wasn't. How would he hide?

She ground into him as he filled the condom and grabbed him tighter like she was milking him for everything she could get. He pulled out and without a word she slipped into the bathroom. He remembered saying something like, "OK then, I'll see you later. Meeting in the theater at six...," as he and the condom left to rejoin his friends.

"She was pretty hot," a scuba instructor said as Squire sat back down to await the next guest arrival.

"Yeah," he replied as the condom began to droop. "I'll be right back, I need to piss."

He saw her three days later. Her sun induced reddening was beginning to brown up as she sat on the steps of the nightclub quietly crying. He sat down next to her and slipped his arm around her shoulder. She pushed him away, "Sorry, I just don't want to be touched right now."

"You OK?" Squire asked.

"No, I hate my boyfriend and he is going to propose to me when I get back…"

CHAPTER 14

"The defense calls Miss Veronica Mancini," Mason announced.

Squire looked at her wondering if that was really her. He stretched his memory to picture what she had been like, remembering the curve of her hips and her bare back better than her face. She was still cute but... "Huh," he said quietly. Something about this witness didn't seem right. The way she walked, her mannerisms weren't anything like the others but what did he know? But for a brief encounter, he barely knew her. It had been a struggle just to remember her first name.

"Miss Mancini," Mason beamed. He was proud of this one. The work it took to find her, to convince her that there was more to this trial than a few angry husbands out for blood. "Please tell the court how you and Mr. McDermott met."

"We met at a resort in the Caribbean, in Turks and Caicos. I was going through a lot of things then. Squire was sort of the thing I needed in my life at that moment."

"Could you explain what it was that you needed?"

"I needed time to think. Then when I saw him, I knew I needed to get fucked by that hot guy," she blurted out.

Judge Perkins leaned over towards her, "Miss Mancini, please. We have had too much of this sort of explicit content in this courtroom. Please measure your responses to a PG-Rating."

"Sorry, Judge," she capitulated. "We had intercourse."

"Better," Judge Perkins smiled.

"And Miss Mancini," Mason continued, "who initiated? Who came on to whom?"

"That was me for sure. I didn't give him much choice. I just stuck my vagina practically in his face and he did what he was supposed to." The gallery erupted. The gavel slammed followed by a stern glare from the judge.

"Sorry Judge," she said again. "I showed him my lady parts in a seductive, come-hither manner and he was a good boy and obliged."

"Thank you, sweetheart," Judge Perkins smiled again. He seemed relatively taken by this one, "but this room is not a comedy club. Mr. Braddock, control your witnesses and questioning or I will hold *you* in contempt."

Woodrow P. Devine was suspiciously quiet, his coffee mug rest on his stomach between nervous slurping. Mason noticed when descriptions of sexual content pushed the limits, Woodrow got weird and anxious as if he were about to run to the bathroom.

"Miss Mancini, how long had you known Squire McDermott before you and he engaged in intercourse?"

She paused and began to laugh. Squire watched thinking that this woman had no sense of shame. She didn't care at all what people thought of her. "Um, if I had to guess it was about forty seconds, definitely less than a minute.

"I find that hard to believe, Miss Mancini," Mason replied.

"Oh, it's true. He carried my suitcase to my room and I pounced on him. Last man I ever had sex with."

The whole courtroom went silent as if they were all deep in calculation. The last *man* she had sex with. Was she? She had no stereotypical signs for what they all thought. Where was the club issued haircut? Everyone was thinking Subaru but she looked BMW. She had the appearance of an ex high school cheerleader, retaining that look well into her thirties.

"If you don't mind, what is your sexual orientation, Miss Mancini," Mason asked.

"Oh, I'm a lesbian. In fact, I am married. That's my wife sitting over there." An almost prettier woman waved from the gallery.

"And all this happened after your interlude with Mr. McDermott?" Mason asked.

"He didn't have anything to do with it, if that's what you mean. He was there at the time when I needed something or someone to snap me out of the life I thought I should be living. I was a mess and I really needed him right then, right there. And it wasn't the sex as much as it was him.

"I remember later in the week when I was feeling really guilty for what I was going to do to my boyfriend when I got home. Squire sat with me and talked like he was a real friend and cared. It was really sweet. He would be the guy I would want if I wanted guys. The boy could…," she paused and looked timidly up at the judge, "um, he was really good at what he did. "

Mason turned towards the plaintiffs. His eyes hesitated on Victoria and Meagan. He could see that Veronica's comment was resonating with them. But before passing her off to Woodrow he had one more question, "Would you characterize Squire McDermott as a temporary solution to temporary female problems?"

"Objection, most definitely leading, Your Honor," Woodrow P. Devine complained.

"Sustained, Mr. Braddock. Rephrase the question."

"No further questions, Your Honor," Mason grinned.

"Miss or is it Mrs. Mancini?" Woodrow P. Devine bellowed.

"Miss is fine."

"Miss Mancini, are you telling the court that you and the defendant engaged in coitus within a few moments of meeting? It seems to me that almost any man would have been up to the task."

"I'm sure almost all men would think they would," she replied.

"Then the choice of Mr. McDermott was made merely because he was there and you needed something, was it not, Miss Mancini?"

"Not at all, I had no intentions of just doing that with any available man. I was at the resort the whole week. He was the only one I hooked up with and I had plenty of offers. It was him. When I think about him after all these years, I remember how he was, how he made me feel right from the beginning. It was like something animalistic took over me and I had to have him. He gave me the only orgasm I have ever gotten from a man."

"You said you had a boyfriend who was planning to propose around the time of your encounter with Mr. McDermott," Devine went on.

"I did," she replied.

"What came of that?"

"I went home, told him I had just fucked the most beautiful man I had ever met and I couldn't marry him." Judge Perkins stared at her, his hand reached for the gavel. "Sorry, Judge," she apologized quickly. "Squire is innocent in all this. I don't think he really understands."

"The jury will disregard Miss Mancini's last comment," Judge Perkins sighed.

"It doesn't sound like you know much of anything about Squire McDermott," Devine growled. "How could you in the time you had with him?"

"Objection, Your Honor. Extemporaneous rambling and or badgering the witness," Mason complained.

"Sustained."

Devine stared down at his notes searching for something to pin down Squire McDermott as a ruthless cad but she was not the one to know. Somehow she had turned him into a convenient, albeit desirable tool, almost lifeless unless animated by a woman. *That's it! Squire McDermott is a dildo*, his head raced. *He is a tool. Now, how do I throw him in the trash?*

"Mr. Devine, unless you have something pressing right now, the court will take a recess until 1:00 PM," Judge Perkins spoke up.

"That's fine, Your Honor."

Mason pointed towards a table near a large potted tree they could hide Squire behind in case the gallery came to gawk. She had taken his hand as they walked down the block and said almost nothing. Mason walked behind watching her look up at Squire. The affection she had for him was obvious. Veronica's wife took his other hand.

"So, you are him?" the wife asked.

"Yes, Ali. This is Squire," Veronica answered. Squire was getting the impression they were up to something.

"What is *it*?" Mason interrupted.

Alison leaned into Mason, nearly touching foreheads. "What?" she asked.

"*It*, the other day in court the subject came up that Squire *just gets it* but nobody can tell us what *it* is. Not definitively, anyway."

Alison thought a moment, "That's easy, a guy who just *gets it* is one who intuitively understands a woman's emotional and sexual needs without trying, without thinking, just being. It's like he was born to be a woman but made man by some quirk of nature. He is a spiritual hermaphrodite. If you couple that with emotional and physical strength and good looks, he is absolutely one in tens of millions. As a woman, you have to breed with it. If you are into that sort of thing...," she said as she reached for Veronica's hand. "We both used to be but I love Veronica. You, my love?" Veronica nodded.

"I get the impression that Squire is a pariah to some people, especially other men. What do you think?" Mason asked.

Veronica took over, "I don't know. He and I had an amazing quickie. It was impetuous and raw. I don't regret it at all. In fact, I would say it brought me to where I am now. Some women don't feel grounded until they stomp on something so hard their feet hurt. Squire was like my concrete floor.

"I hid from him at the resort because I knew all I would do was fuck him constantly and not really think about why I was there. It all came together outside the nightclub when he sat down next to me. I was crying my eyes out, in pain, and he just wanted me to feel happy. He had no other motive. Most men can't do anything for a woman without some sort of secret plan to fuck her later."

She looked at Squire, "What do you think about when you are inside a woman and she is coming?"

He thought; he didn't know. It just all came together at the time. He loved to watch a woman cum. He loved to watch her go from a feral, aggressive creature, to being taken over by ghostlike ecstasy before coming back down to earth as a soft, serene soul full of affection who felt safe and secure in his arms. The polarity of fucking and feeling was like a drug to him. The only thing he didn't understand was why it wouldn't last. What made women throw him away as fast as they threw themselves at him? It made him feel like he wasn't real regardless of how hard he was trying to be.

* * *

THE JURY FILED IN. Woodrow P. Devine cleared his throat. It was a gurgling clamor the room had grown used to. "Miss Mancini," he paused and paused a little more. Mason rolled his eyes, Judge Perkins caught him, squinting his dismay with Mason down from above. "Miss Mancini, do you suspect that Mr. McDermott may have slipped you something?"

"Objection!" Mason stared at the judge.

"Mr. Devine! Do I need to list the reasons for Mr. Braddock's objection?" Judge Perkins yelled from the bench.

"No, Your Honor, I believe the list is extensive," Devine succumbed.

"Proceed, then."

"Miss Mancini, could it have been possible that Mr. Devine slipped you something like a sexual stimulant or something of the sort?"

"No, the only thing I had was a margarita on the plane," she replied.

"Uh-oh," Mason whispered.

"Did you feel inebriated when you met Mr. McDermott?"

Mason clenched up. This was going wrong. *Fucking Woodrow*, he thought.

"Maybe a little but there was more than two hours or more between the margarita and the sex."

"Did he tell you that he was a bartender? Did he say anything like, 'meet me at the bar where I work' so he could ply you with more drinks?"

She thought, " No, not at the time. I don't understand why that would matter anyway. I was on vacation."

Devine paused to redirect. "When did you see him next?" Devine asked.

"I saw him behind the bar later that night," Veronica replied.

"And you didn't approach him. Were you embarrassed?"

"Why would I be embarrassed?" she countered.

"Please answer the question," Devine continued.

"No, I wasn't embarrassed." Veronica was rattled. Things were turning for the plaintiffs. Howard and Stephen leaned in while their wives sat unaffected.

Say it, Woodrow. Say something stupid like normal, you idiot, Mason thought.

"Did you have a strong father figure growing up?"

Yes! Mason thought. "Objection! He is making assumptions as to the someone's sexual motivations based on family history."

"Overruled."

"What?" Mason yelled.

"Overruled! Sit down Mr. Braddock!" Judge Perkins looked like he was ready to brandish a revolver everyone assumed he had behind the bench.

"You may answer, Miss Mancini."

"My father left when I was very young."

Woodrow P. Devine looked at Veronica affecting concern as if he were taking on the patriarchal role he assumed she needed. He and all the good, upright men could bring this country back together if and when people saw what they had to offer.

It took everything Mason had to keep himself from inducing vomiting. Squire doodled, looking up periodically to smile at Veronica. He seemed to be looking forward to his fate: single and penniless with a court-ordered garnishment everywhere he went.

Squire turned towards the gallery searching the faces for Alison. When he locked eyes with her, she winked. Maybe things weren't so bad. It felt nice to be understood by someone.

"Miss Mancini, I thank you," Woodrow P. Devine nuzzled up. "No further questions."

* * *

VERONICA, Squire and Alison sat on his couch eating omelets. The sunrise beamed through the window. All was quiet except for the occasional scrape of a fork against his mother's old china, the slurp of coffee, and contended sighs.

CHAPTER 15

"Dr. Markowitz, thank you for coming."

"It's my pleasure, Mr. Braddock," Dr. Jason E. Markowitz replied.

"Could you the share your credentials with the court?"

"Sure, I am Dr. Jason Markowitz. I have a Ph.D. in Psychology from the University of Notre Dame. I specialize in counseling men and women in their relationship struggles and have been in practice for about twenty years. I am licensed in this state as well as others."

"And Lilly Hakobyan is a patient of yours?" Mason asked.

"She has been, yes. We have had many sessions."

"And you have a client consent letter from her?"

Dr. Markowitz shifted in his seat. "I do, she has given me carte blanche to discuss her reasons for seeking counseling," he answered. "She waives all client privilege. It's in the document."

"This document?" Mason waved the papers, dropping a copy on the plaintiffs' table and handing another to the bailiff.

"Dr. Markowitz, please share with the court why Miss Lilly Zabelle Hakobyan came to see you."

He seemed calm, relaxed as he leaned into the microphone. "Miss Hakobyan was under the impression she was enchanted, as if some sort of spirit had taken over her physical being. This spirit would come to her in the night." Dr. Markowitz paused and cleared his throat, "She would wake up with an intense sensation of orgasm."

"That is how she described it? An intense sensation?" Mason asked.

"It was more than that, she described all of the physical attributes of a real orgasm such as involuntary muscles spasms and heavy breathing."

"Is it common to dream yourself into sexual satisfaction, wet dreams I think they are called."

"It is much more common in men but a significant percentage of them happen for women," Dr. Markowitz replied.

Mason stepped around the lectern and walked up to the jury box to take a look. They were wide awake. "Dr. Markowitz if this is common, why would Miss Hakobyan pursue counseling?"

"Because her dreams were always about a particular man, Squire McDermott. She was convinced she was being haunted by him specifically. In our sessions, we discussed her need for connection and closeness. It was something she had described that she felt in him. But obviously, it was something that was nearly impossible to obtain. He was more of an idea for her, a projection for her psyche. Someone who had penetrated her deeply on a spiritual level.

"I have noticed this in some other cases, and I think it is widely known, that within the first months of a romantic relationship we are with the person we want to see. It is beyond that initial projection that relationship becomes reality, as it were."

Mason paced, "What was the problem with this projection?"

"It was, as I said, a fabrication of her desires."

"So, are you saying that in Miss Hakobyan's case, she could not see Squire McDermott past the initial projection phase? Like he just ceased to exist?"

"For the most part... For her needs, he exists only in the realm of intense sexual desire and is limited to that. It's unfortunate for men like Squire McDermott who cannot seem to break through into reality. This is conjecture but I believe that it is possible that women look at them as fun but not something to keep. I would liken it to buying a season pass at a theme park. You have expectations of going frequently then the reality hits and you stop riding the rides. They become routine and lose the thrill you found in them when they were a new experience."

"Are you saying that Squire McDermott is like a fun ride for women?"

"From my discussions with Miss Hakobyan, that would be an accurate comparison and an unfortunate reality for Mr. McDermott, assuming he would have liked to pursue something more."

"What if Mr. McDermott could make a solid case for continuing a relationship past this fun phase and into the reality phase?" Dr. Markowitz hesitated to answer, "Dr. Markowitz?" Mason prodded.

"In my clinical experience, it is exceptionally rare for a man to be naturally seductive and possess the attributes that a steady, more stereotypical man has. He is usually one or the other. Rather, he is usually the usual not one of the Squire McDermotts of the world.

"And the combination of the two types is so rare that he

would be pursued by hundreds, maybe thousands of women. From what Miss Hakobyan and I discussed about her dreams, Squire McDermott possesses a feral, sexual allure that is most uncommon. He seems to know nothing about these attributes nor how to control them."

"Control them how?" Mason asked.

"By becoming someone he is not. Once he tried to do this, Miss Hakobyan lost her attraction for him. Once he was real, he was discarded. She wanted him for the, lack of a better example, thrill ride. Although they had experienced a strong friendship together before their first sexual experience, she still valued him for his sexuality. In her words, 'he wasn't boyfriend or husband material.'"

Mason turned away from Dr. Markowitz to catch Stephen Rogers and Howard Cullen leering at their wives with contemptuous superiority. He knew what they were thinking: Squire McDermott wasn't a real man. They were real; they could create things that lasted. Squire was a toy meant for girls. Their wives were serious women: refined by the men they had chosen, experience, and age.

Squire was a phase, a lecherous cad waiting for momentary weakness. He and men like him should be reviled. The trial would vindicate their efforts and the energy they put into making it work.

What is a man without effort? Howard Cullen thought. *He is a predator with too much time on his hands and too little focus on the big picture.*

"Dr. Markowitz, is Squire McDermott a player? Someone whose only pursuit is the conquest?"

"If I had ever had a chance to sit with him, maybe I would know for sure but from Miss Hakobyan's sessions it does not appear that he was."

"What was it about him," Mason continued, "that makes you believe he was not?"

"Well, for starters Lilly left him. It was her choice. Wouldn't a player get his satisfaction and vacate?"

"Thank you, Dr. Markowitz," Mason ended. "Your Honor, I have no further questions."

Woodrow P. Devine held up the document giving Dr. Markowitz authority to speak on Lilly's behalf, "Is this document real?"

"Objection, Your Honor! It is clearly notarized and by the court's own notary if I might add," Mason interrupted.

"Sustained, Mr. Devine; the document is real. What are you trying to prove?"

"Your Honor," Devine stumbled, "I... I apologize and will proceed with further questioning."

Wow, Mason thought, he put his hand out blindly to pull Squire into a whisper. He grasped again and felt nothing. He looked, there he sat scribbling in the legal pad like always.

Squire looked up at Mason, "I know what you are going to say," and went back to drawing a beach with footsteps leading to a solitary man in the distance.

"Dr. Markowitz, tell us again why Lilly Hakobyan ended the relationship with Squire McDermott," Devine prodded.

"She did not have a specific reason. It was something she said that she felt at the time. She indicated that she had plans for herself, for her future, and could not see Squire in them."

"If Squire McDermott is so fulfilling to women, why can't he seem to keep one?" Devine smirked.

"I don't know. I have not had the opportunity to counsel him and obviously I don't see that ever happening, at least in this lifetime."

Woodrow P. Devine looked agitated, "And why should we believe anything about a man who cannot even stand up for himself and adapt to the world as it is?"

"Objection!" Mason yelled.

"Mr. Devine, do not badger," Judge Perkins scolded. "Do you have any relevant questions for this witness?"

"Yes, Your Honor," Woodrow sulked.

"Dr. Markowitz, do you believe that Miss Hakobyan was in a phase of her life that Mr. McDermott may have exploited for his own pleasure?"

"I do not. I believe she exploited him for her own pleasure." The gallery began to whisper.

* * *

"I THINK I'm going to have to fuck my civil procedure professor," Brittany sighed. "Squire, why did you come here?"

"For moments like this," he grinned. They lay by the pool naked. He watched it move and shift. It seemed to animate whenever he was out full frontal in the sun. It shrank and expanded never seeming to find a comfortable position for itself.

Brittany leaned over to watch, "Why does it do that?"

"I think it really likes the sun. It gets all squirmy and happy. Can't sit still," he replied.

"It's getting hard again."

"You're staring at it. It's armoring itself against an impending attack." Brittany laughed as she tossed her hair to the side and kneeled next him. Her mouth closed over him at the precipice of his totem. Her eyes tilted upwards into his as she stroked then licked. She watched, waiting for him to succumb but he held steadfast against her. She took all of him she could. Those eyes flickered up again. Still nothing. He sat, arms behind his head watching her.

She pushed him forward, her mouth found the base and its two partners. She tickled them. First one with her hand then the other she swallowed whole bouncing it around in her mouth like a peach pit. Her tongue flattened against the underside and slithered up and off then along his stomach to his chest. "I am so fucking wet right now," she whispered in his ear as his hands pushed her down onto him.

"Oh," she cried with surprise. "Oh my god, you are in so deep."

For Squire the comment had more meaning than she would ever know. He loved her. They had been friends for years. In his suitcase there was a ring, but deep in his soul he knew what would happen if he gave it to her.

Her rigid nipples raked across his chest, any harder and he thought they would draw blood. There was something he did to her. Something she said no other man had. She came alive on him in a way he knew couldn't last nor be replicated. "Fuck me, Squire. I want to feel you. You can cum in me, remember? I want to feel it."

She was one he had to concentrate for. There was something about her he couldn't explain; he knew she was *the one* if not for the circumstances. Maybe it was the impossibility of them – the religious and economic backstories that define lives and forbid passions. All he could think of was the years they had spent like this; it was all a bit of a tease until the inevitable. As she kissed at his neck, his distant thoughts had taken over for what concentration had so frequently required. "You haven't cum yet," she panted. "Oh my god, this is so good. Fuck."

He could barely hear her through the raging dialog in his head. It was over. Or at least it would be over sometime soon. The smacking, sweaty slap of her ass against his thighs, her breasts catching him in the chin, he was distant and she was enthralled. He knew he would have to end it and send her away to her destiny.

He thought about whether he should finally start dating one of the girls she kept presenting to him. Maybe that was how deeply she loved him and how afraid she was to abandon generations. She was matchmaking a suitable substitute to placate two realities. His mind was lost as she came again and dropped onto her lounge, panting under the climbing late morning sun. In a time of youth, open and free, they were a fling that started a thing that could never be. Regardless of their chemistry, this was all they would be.

"Remember when we fucked behind the meerkats at the zoo? I can still see those big, round eyes staring at me," she laughed. She looked over at Squire, his eyes hidden behind his sunglasses, the rest of him distant. "Are you OK?" she asked.

"I'm fine," he said as he stood. He reached down and took her chin and kissed her for the last time.

* * *

"How does a woman exploit a man for pleasure? That seems absurd," Devine mocked.

"In many ways," Dr. Markowitz answered, "as I am sure you know, women can be very manipulative. It's how they fight. It is part of their nature and a man will succumb to it and cower before it. A well-adjusted, normal man recoils in the face of a woman's heartless and even abusive words where in a damaged man it could incite violence. It is normal for a man to appear weak in front of a screaming woman. He wants to fix her problem, to ease her pain. His mind begins to race with solutions the moment she begins to attack him.

"If she continues to badger him, he can only step away. A deeply troubled man, strikes out at her. A man with internal strength stays firm in what he believes is right and walks away from her when he can do nothing else. If she comes back, she has realized he is worth keeping. But I am getting away from the original question...

"It is a well-worn idiom that it is a woman's prerogative

to change her mind. In reality, she has a duty to herself and her survival to change her mind when she is feeling unsure of the future."

Devine grinned, "So, that's what it is. Squire McDermott's long list of conquests are just women changing their mind and growing up?"

"Objection!"

"What is your objection, Mr. Braddock?" Judge Perkins asked.

"He's leading, making up value judgements for the witness."

"Your Honor," Woodrow P. Devine huffed, "it is a rhetorical question that was to be followed up before Mr. Braddock interrupted.

"Then follow up, Mr. Devine," Judge Perkins shot back.

"The women were, for lack of a better phrase, growing up. Is that what you observed, Dr. Markowitz?"

"I think the phrase *growing up* is loaded with social implications and, to some degree, virtue signaling. It partitions women into segments that are mutually exclusive of each other and ignores the whole of her experiences that create who she is. We do not necessarily progress through life by defined starts and stops in phases.

"Everything we are and do is dragged along with us. For instance, think of what you may envision of yourself as you enter the gates of the next world after death, if you believe in such things. Do you see yourself as the hunched-over old man or the young, strong man you once were? Does a woman see the grey, the wrinkles? I would suggest not. I believe, and have some evidence, that we tend to think of ourselves at the point we remember as being at our best."

"Can't one get stuck in that thought?" Devine interrupted.

"Certainly," Dr. Markowitz replied, "there is a separation between what is current and real and what is historical and, for the most part, fictional. But the past is drawn on and carried because it was real, the future only beholds hope."

"And the present?"

"Ah, the present," Dr. Markowitz exhaled, "that is a blip of time when we are either contented or allowing ourselves to be distracted with needless anxiety."

"What do you believe someone like Squire McDermott hoped for in all of his conquests?" Devine asked.

"Love."

CHAPTER 16

"Good morning," Judge Perkins looked like he had slept well. Maybe he could feel the end of the trial nearing. Whatever it was, he seemed happy. "Mr. Braddock," he smiled down from the bench, "call your witness."

"Thank you, Judge," Mason grinned. "The defense calls Meagan Rogers."

"Objection!" Woodrow P. Devine shouted. "He can't call her. She'll plead the fifth!" Woodrow turned on her, "You're going to plead the fifth, Mrs. Rogers."

"Ahem," Judge Perkins gurgled, "would you like me to explain adverse inference to our jury now or after lunch, Mr. Devine?"

"Meagan?" Stephen Rogers blurted out. "Why?"

"Truth, Stephen," she whispered as she stood to be sworn in.

Nothing had ruined Judge Perkins morning so far, not even this. He was still somewhat taken by how good his coffee tasted. He seemed amused and anxious to see where

Mason was going with this potentially hostile witness. Devine sulked, providing yet another amusement.

"Mrs. Rogers, thank you," Mason began. She nodded and smiled back, her eyes flicked quickly towards her husband and locked on Victoria. Howard Cullen noticed. "Could you remind the court as to the circumstances of your and Squire McDermott's first meeting?"

She felt a little tingle as she thought back to that night, "I went out to get a drink. Stephen and the children were in Rhode Island at his mother's for a few weeks and I was feeling lonely and isolated in our house. It was so quiet I just felt like I had to go somewhere. So I went. I had no intentions of meeting anyone. Squire was working at the bar."

He looked up from his doodling long enough to see her look his way then out over the gallery like she was searching for something. The affair had lasted long enough to pick up the quirks of her feelings and he liked them, all of them. To Squire, Meagan was almost too adorable. There had to be something wrong with her. Everything had seemed to go too smoothly right from the start, until...

"Did Mr. McDermott seduce you or coerce you in any way that night?"

"No, he got my number then asked me to meet him for a drink at another bar. I went. It was my choice to go," Stephen Rogers' hand smashed down on the table. The judge glared while Woodrow P. Devine tried to calm him. The gavel struck again.

Meagan looked timid and ashamed but somehow she sat up straight as if the truth was more important to her now than anything else. "It was like a date but there was something about it. It almost felt like I was on a different spiritual plane with him."

Veronica Cullen began to nod in solidarity. She knew

exactly what Meagan was talking about. His touch was ethereal. She felt a tingle run down her spine into her pelvis, then a subtle wave of motion seemed to rise up out of her chair rocking her hips in gentle circles. "Ooh," a whimper slipped out.

Howard Cullen turned to Victoria, "Is there something wrong with you?"

She looked into her husband's eyes, breathed in deeply and mouthed, "Squire." A hand slid between her legs. Before she could touch herself, she realized where she was. A look of surprise and dread fell over her like a veil. "No, no. Nothing's wrong," she replied hastily.

"How long were you at the second bar, the date bar?" Mason asked.

"One drink, not even. I don't think Squire even touched his Scotch, maybe a sip. I couldn't smell it on his breath."

"You were close enough at this first date to smell his breath?" Mason looked up from his notes.

"Absolutely, he kissed me," she replied.

"How long were you with him before he kissed you?" Mason asked.

"I don't know, maybe five minutes?"

"You don't recall exactly?" Mason asked.

Meagan's chest heaved taking in a breath, "I was in a dream. I was overwhelmed by him, his scent, his eyes, his body… I had no concept of time."

For the pent up heat emitting from Meagan, Stephen's energy countered hers. He looked as though he were between sobbing and wanting kill someone. Howard Cullen sat rigid, arms crossed, analyzing the situation and wondering what it was that Squire McDermott had done to damage his Victoria. What were the unspeakable sexual acts she was hiding? If he did them with Meagan, he probably did them with his wife. For now, all he could do was curse that man's soul to hell where it belonged and destroy whatever life he might have left.

"Mrs. Rogers, without going into too much specific detail, let me ask you about Squire McDermott's sexual appetite."

"Objection! How is this relevant, Your Honor?"

"Judge Perkins, this is a trial about a law that punishes infidelity in order to protect the sanctity of marriage. One of the primary benefits of marriage for a man and I am assuming for a woman, although I can't speak directly to that, is convenient access to sexual gratification. The nature of the sexual act is important to its perceived value," Mason defended.

"Overruled," Judge Perkins thumped. "Proceed, Mr. Braddock." Woodrow P. Devine flopped back into his chair.

"Mrs. Rogers, was there anything beyond standard coitus, given the variety of creative contortions, that Squire McDermott liked?"

"He liked blowjobs," Meagan replied. "I guess that's sort of nonstandard and he really liked to go down on me. He was really good at it..." She yanked at a button to shake some breeze into her blouse thinking about it.

* * *

"Lay back," he told her as he slipped his hand up towards her mouth. Her lips closed on two of his fingers as his tongue worked its way up her thigh. She could feel him tracing her. Any moment she would feel him but he kept her waiting. The tongue teased. It was almost unbearable. She wanted him to just do it but the wait was making her so horny, so wet she couldn't protest. All she could manage was to suck on his fingers as if they were made to transmit signals to his mouth. "Uh," she whimpered as he found the spot. He felt strong even in this vulnerable place he had put himself. She took in his fingers one more time before she reached down to run her hands through his hair.

He flicked his tongue just at the right rhythm. As she moaned and wriggled. He stayed constant. How did he know she liked that? He seemed to be reading her mind or maybe he was so connected to what she wanted his instincts guided him. Whatever it was, she had never felt this from a man. He wasn't trying, he was just there for her doing the thing without rushing, without forcing anything. Her fingernails bit into his scalp. He didn't flinch. Slowly he began to pick up the pace– so slowly. How did he know?

She felt herself along a journey that started out as an idea, then a step, then a march, then into a full sprint. She was losing herself, her breasts heaved upwards, he dug in harder. She grabbed at the sheets and ground herself into his mouth. With a deep, exhausted breath, she sank into the bed. She felt him inside her. When had he? As one, they rolled gently. She was on top of him, riding him how she wanted as he pumped on her from below.

Then as she collapsed, he held her close to him. She tensed and quivered against him, surrounding him, feeling him deep inside. She felt her body meld against his, her pelvis shook uncontrollably. The sheet came up over her. She felt its warmth. She felt protected. She rolled over onto her side and slipped off into sleep with him still inside her.

When she awoke, they were apart. He was gone; the comforter was tucked around her. An aroma of cooking came from the kitchen. She thought about trying to get out of bed to help him. The door opened, his smile lit the room. He was wearing boxers. "Oh god, that body," she whispered as he slid in next to her. A fork full for her, and one for him until it was gone. They slipped back deep into the sheets.

* * *

"Did Squire McDermott ever try anything sexually you didn't want to do?" Mason asked.

"No, we never talked about what I wanted. He just knew. Whatever he gave me, I wanted."

"Is this similar to your experience with Mr. Rogers?" Meagan froze. This was going to be it. If she answered, that was it. They could never recover from this. "Mrs. Rogers?" Mason pushed.

"Um, it is not similar." She couldn't look at her husband. She tried to find someone in the room who looked sympathetic. That girl reporter, towards the back. She had to know. Meagan fixated on Monica Beaumont. "Stephen always tells me what he wants in detail. He says other men get those things and so should he. He says that a lot."

"Does he expect to get what he wants?" Mason asked. Monica Beaumont's head snapped up, locking eyes with what looked like a traumatized woman staring at her.

"Yes," Meagan replied, "he expects me to do what he wants. If I don't, he will be very moody. Sometimes for weeks."

"Would he be abusive? Violent?"

"No, he just stops talking to me like I don't exist," Meagan answered.

"That is a form of abuse, Mrs. Rogers," Mason countered.

"Objection! He is not qualified to make that assertion," Devine yelled.

"Sustained. Mr. Braddock, stay within your limits," Judge Perkins lectured.

"Did it feel abusive to be ostracized, Mrs. Rogers?" Mason asked cautiously.

"It did, and I didn't like being talked about."

"Can you elaborate on *being talked about*?" Mason had been given an opportunity.

"At the country club, the men all talk. They drink and

they talk, or brag about what they can get their wives to do. It's like a game for them to see what sort of things…" Meagan froze. She had opened up a hole she would have to climb back out of but something told her to dig.

"She knows," she went on, pointing at Victoria. "They all talk about it, anal seems to be their favorite. I guess some women like it. I don't. I hate it but I had to do it. I felt forced just so he could be part of the club and for his big, fat, fucking ego!"

"Order!" Judge Perkins pounded. "Order!" Control was slipping away again. "Mrs. Rogers, no more outbursts!"

"I am sorry, Your Honor," behind a shadow of momentary fear she knew she had hit Stephen directly where he needed it. He had to know he would never measure up to Squire's touch, the feeling of his heartbeat against her chest, the way he enraptured her, the unforgettable memory of a place inside her she could never deny nor regret.

"Mrs. Rogers, I think we are about done," Mason looked up at her. "Thank you for your honesty from both myself and Squire. I have one last question." The whole courtroom tensed. "If your connection to Squire was so deep, so spiritual and fulfilling why not leave your husband and pursue Squire for something long-term?"

Woodrow P. Devine grinned. All was not lost.

Meagan's realization of the truth hit her hard. It wasn't anything Squire had done. It was the circumstance of her life, the one she chose. She felt imprisoned by the world and her natural instincts.

"It was the reason I married Stephen. When we met, I was a young nurse. I saw how men acted in their weakest state. They would be lying there dying and still looking at me like I was a sex object right up until they took their last breath. I learned very young that the female body can control men to get what we want. I wanted everything and society was telling me I could have everything. But that's a lie. When I got pregnant with my first child, I realized how vulnerable I was. We weren't married yet. I was going to be a single mother or married. Thankfully, Stephen wanted to get married even thought he knew the child wasn't his." The courtroom gasped.

"He stepped in for the other man. It was honorable. But I came to realize that he always regretted that decision. He secretly resented me for it even though we went on to have two more children together and lead a mostly happy family life. Because of all the regret, he became very controlling over the years. Sex for him seemed to be like retaliation. We never really connected. When I met Squire, I was like a girl again. But I couldn't keep him because the reality was, I had become a woman."

The courtroom clock ticked away the seconds. Mason didn't know what to do. The only sound came from the uneasy rustling of the plaintiffs' bodies trying to adjust themselves and find consolation in anything but going forward.

"No further questions, Your Honor," Mason finally broke the silence.

"Mr. Devine?"

"We have no questions, Your Honor." Both Stephen and Howard shot stabbing glares at Woodrow. Victoria dabbed at her eyes.

CHAPTER 17

"And what do you think, Mr. Braddock?" Judge Perkins asked.

"I don't particularly care one way or the other what Woodrow says in closing."

"Don't you find it odd, Judge, that Mr. McDermott can't seem to bother with this trial?" Woodrow P. Devine complained.

"You know as well as anyone, Mr. Devine, that in civil court the defendant is not technically required to be here. His counsel is here. I would think this would be to your advantage. I ask, why do you care?"

"I want to see his face up on the stand. There is nothing without that," Woodrow grumbled. "This is the first significant trial involving the Family Unity Sustainment Act and the defendant is checked out."

"I would like to remind you that one of your plaintiffs has abandoned you," Judge Perkins looked up at Woodrow. "If you want to talk about being checked out..." Mason slunk back a step feeling a little laughter coming on.

"And you," the judge shifted, "this has been one of the most debaucherous marathons of bullshit I have had in this courtroom in years. What do you have to say to that, Mr. Braddock?"

"I apologize, Your Honor," Mason sighed. "I see this case as more than who did who and how to whom. I believe this law is unjust and ignores a central component in the courtship and mating habits of humans."

"And what is that?" Woodrow P. Devine snapped.

"Your Honor," Mason looked for permission, "may I explain graphically."

"In my chambers, you may. Out there…"

"There is a central element that the law does not consider," Mason hesitated.

"Spit it out," Woodrow complained.

"What makes for a good husband doesn't necessarily make for a good fuck."

"Ugh, Your Honor!" Woodrow P. Devine reacted. "That's not a legal argument! A good… What he said."

"Don't piss yourself, Mr. Devine," Judge Perkins replied. "You two go do your closings and let's be done with this nonsense."

* * *

Woodrow P. Devine stood before the jury. Little diamonds on the ends of his collar bar glittered beneath his shining teeth. "Ladies and gentlemen of the jury, it is my great pleasure to stand before you and begin the closing of this most wretched trial. I, for one, feel as if I owe you an apology for having to sit through the testimony but if it had not been you, it would have been twelve other strong souls. Not only are we here to bring justice for these two fine families against a cad, a buffoon, a sexual predator who nails hearts on his wall still warm and weeping for whatever elixir he has fed them, but we are here to uphold the law.

"It is the law that brought us here – an enactment that was a long time coming in a hedonistic hothouse of deviance. A law forged from righteousness, the Family Unity Sustainment Act. You have heard the testimony; you have read the law and now you are tasked with upholding the family values this state holds so dear. This nascent act has yet to be tested until now.

"Do I believe there have not been justifiable circumstances to bring other suits to trial?" Woodrow chuckled. "Of course there have. I am not that naive. And neither are you but here we are ready to make what is the right thing to do the good thing to do. Your decision to do what is right will set an example for the citizens of this great state and the states who have followed us into this brave world of virtue in the name of the family – that most holy of institutions this country once turned its back on.

"I ask you, how can we not decide for the victims of Mr. Squire McDermott when he cannot even bring himself to stand for himself? He could show up when lechery was afoot. Why not in his own defense?

"Where is Squire McDermott? Who is Squire McDermott?" Woodrow P. Devine paused; his hand swept over the courtroom. "How can a man who brought tears to these good people, the Rogerses and Cullens, not stand up for himself? That inability to act, in and of itself, shows the cowardice of a man who takes when he sees fit. Like the serpent slithering up to Eve, he deceives and extorts when someone is weakened. Who and what is Squire McDermott? Where is Squire McDermott?

"I don't know where he is anymore than you do but I will tell you what he is – a predator: heartless, infantile, and lecherous. Do your duty and find for these fine people."

Woodrow snapped at his lapels and spun towards his clients.

* * *

"Well, that was a show," Mason laughed. He nudged at Squire.

"We will have an hour recess," Judge Perkins smacked the gavel. Mason stood to stretch out – an hour to get a sandwich and go through his closing one more time.

Squire tapped Mason on the shoulder as they stood, "I'm going to go to the beach."

* * *

The hour flew by. As Mason watched the jury file in, he looked at the empty chair next to him; the notepad and pen were lifeless. *A closing with no defendant,* he thought.

"Mr. Braddock," Judge Perkins said as he gestured towards the jury. Mason stood.

"Ladies and gentlemen, thank you for your patience. As you know and can see for yourselves, my client could not be here but that does not imply and certainly does not prove liability as Mr. Devine would like for you to believe. We all heard the testimony. Underneath all of the drama there is a truth that you hold in your hands and can either express or deny. Who is responsible for one's passions?

"Squire McDermott has been made into a scapegoat for the inadequacies of these two men. He was, as you heard in the testimony, misled as to the marital status of Mrs. Cullen and Mrs. Rogers. He was a toy, a plaything to them. What we are here for and what this law was meant to do is to make scapegoats for an assumption. That assumption is: two people who may have been once passionately in love can and do grow apart and seek other outlets for their passions. The Family Unity Sustainment Act ignores this and was made primarily by men to protect an investment, a delusion of ownership, nothing more.

"But that investment implies that women are, and reduces them to being, property and possession. Under the guise of protecting the family, this law seeks only to control. It is not Squire McDermott who is on trial here, it is the law itself. It was whatever the reality was inside the homes of Howard and Victoria Cullen and Stephen and Meagan Rogers that gave the women reasons to look outside their marriages for something else. Were feelings hurt? I have no doubt.

"But to bring a suit against a man whose nature attracts women without effort, a man who sought love and was used for pleasure, is just a pathetic grasp at ego redemption. Whatever the embarrassment was that the Cullens and Rogers experienced was of their own making. A life of expecting to manage societal perception is a life of persistent chaos. This trial was just that, another attempt at managing perception. It was damage control – the spiteful attack on a man Meagan and Victoria pursued for pleasure.

"Squire McDermott was a tool caught up between the confusion of what is passion and what is duty. They are, and always will be, quite different things. I ask you to exonerate my client and send the Cullens and Rogers and all that come after them a message. Clean your own home before you denigrate another's."

* * *

MASON TAPPED his pen on the table waiting. They had been in the jury room for over an hour. Finally the bailiff appeared and slipped into Judge Perkins' chambers. "All rise…" The jury filed in, the verdict was passed to the judge.

"The plaintiffs have requested that this court poll the jury, Mr. Braddock?"

"Your Honor, no objection."

"Then ladies and gentlemen, please begin with Juror One and reveal your decisions."

"For the plaintiffs, Your Honor. For the plaintiffs, Your Honor. For the plaintiffs, for the defendant."

Mason breathed a sigh of relief, at least one.

"For the defendant, for the plaintiffs, for the plaintiffs, for the defendant, for the defendant, for the plaintiffs, for the defendant. For the defendant, Your Honor."

"A hung jury," Mason whispered. He started to laugh. *What a colossal waste of time*, he thought. Woodrow threw his hands up.

Judge Perkins gaveled the room back to order, "Thank you, jurors, you may leave."

"Your Honor, you aren't going to send them back in?" Woodrow P. Devine complained.

"Mr. Devine, seeing that you have already lost a plaintiff and you have failed to get the required minimum, I am declaring a mistrial. Court is adjourned."

* * *

"Such a beautiful day," Squire sighed contentedly. The waves lapped at the sand. The sun on his chest felt rejuvenating. Everything had been laid out before him – what he was and had always been. *Maybe this is what my soul was looking for*, he thought. *The purpose I served here...*

He felt it in every part of him, and for now it ached, but knowing who he was to women... Maybe knowing was what he needed. Maybe it was meant to free him.

"Hi."

Squire looked up at her glowing in the sun, "Hi," he smiled back.

"May I?" she asked as she sat down on the sand facing him. Her eyes darted and flickered around as she drew her legs in, her hands reached out to take his. "You have a beautiful aura."

"You can see that?" he asked.

"Of course, Squire McDermott," she winked. He felt himself drawn in, his heart slowed to a quiet, steady rhythm. "I am here to take you back."

ABOUT THE AUTHOR

Richard Light is the author of psychological and vigilante fiction that examines the tension between justice, morality, and human endurance. With a focus on character-driven storytelling and moral complexity, his work challenges readers to confront the gray areas of right and wrong.

richardlightbooks.com

ALSO BY RICHARD LIGHT

The King's Game Chapter Two Aristocracy
The King's Game
Killer Interviewing

www.ingramcontent.com/pod-product-compliance
Lightning Source LLC
LaVergne TN
LVHW041843070526
838199LV00045BA/1420